THE RIPPER CLUB

Published 2020

A grisly murder sets computer hacker, Chris, and psychology student, Emma, on the trail of a serial killer and the discovery of the mysterious Ripper Club. Their investigations take them back to Whitechapel 1888 and Jack the Ripper. As the story unfolds and the suspense builds, the connections between the past and the present are revealed. Can they identify the killer before it is too late?

Includes the short supernatural story "Stranger in the Night".

Dedicated to my mother and father

Re-printed June 2020

Prologue

The night was cold and dark, the rain driving down relentlessly against the ground as a lone female figure walked quickly along the deserted street wishing she was home. Her high heels making progress difficult but the £500 in her handbag raising her spirits. At least the cleansing rain washed away the memory of the men from whom she had acquired her bounty. It wasn't so difficult, mainly boring, like milking cows. Infinitely more profitable than working in a bar with all the sleazy innuendo that you are forced to smile politely at while inwardly wanting to punch people in the face. It wasn't even something to be ashamed of. Plenty of her fellow students earned money on phone sex lines or web cams. You didn't even need to leave your bedroom and the money would come tumbling in. Put on sexy panties and stockings and wiggle a bit. She had started that way, moving provocatively in front of her webcam but had been seduced by the greater monetary gains of moving into the world of the physical. It wasn't as difficult as she had initially thought. A friend had introduced her to a woman who operated from her flat, a 50-50 split of money taken and you were good. The only downside being the walk home, especially like now in the October rain. Still she could take a short cut through the park. Although there was no lighting, it was quicker.

As she turned into the park and walked along the narrow tree lined path it seemed even darker than usual tonight, almost foreboding. Probably just the cloud cover, and yet. She was just scaring herself but she did quicken her pace. What's that moving in the shadows? Jesus sometimes the imagination runs wild, like looking under the bed as a young child to make sure the bogeyman is not there. But bad things do happen. Not the ethereal bogeyman obviously but real men with evil in their hearts. They certainly existed, Fred West, Ted Bundy. Stop. Best to put those thoughts out of her mind. Too late, she had freaked herself out. This was eerie. The shadows definitely were moving and getting closer. She wanted to run, but impossible in these bloody stilettos.

She could see a light ahead, the street outside the park. Is that the sound of footsteps behind? A quick look around. Nothing. Just get to the streetlight, safety. So near. There is somebody here. Jesus, get the hell out of here. She quickened her step, almost into a run, get to the light. There's something behind. Don't look round, get to the light. It's close, run, run for your life. All too late she felt the steely grip around her throat and the cold sharp metal penetrate her body.

Chapter 1

Chris Walker sat in the refectory at University College London. It was quiet at this time in the morning, most students at lectures or tutorials. He toyed with his breakfast while leafing through the daily newspaper. Inside there was a brief news item about the body of a young woman that had been found in Regent's Park in the early hours of the morning. He contemplated that it was a basic instinct of man to kill, the reasons being varied and myriad but nonetheless the basic impulse resides within us all. Too much of it not to be the case, a daily occurrence in any country you care to mention. Revenge, money, love, just because you like it. Take your pick on the reasons to kill.

- Penny for your thoughts. Emma had sat down in front of him though he had been oblivious, lost in his own thoughts.

Emma O'Neil, like Chris, was a final year student at UCL. Unlike Chris, who was studying computer programming, Emma was reading psychology. He had met Emma through his flatmate Liam Davies who also studied psychology. They had been working on a project together so she was often in their flat. Emma was naturally pretty with her emerald green eyes and auburn hair that was styled in a bob. She wore minimal make-up and jewellery, only an antique heart-shaped silver locket around her neck which she often complained was sealed closed. Chris had liked her almost at once. She was quite outgoing and had many friends. Chris new this because they had become friends on Facebook almost immediately. He knew of her popularity because she had over 400 friends. Chris had 6. This did not overly worry Chris as how could anyone have 400 friends, that was spreading yourself pretty thin. There was clearly a big difference between a social media friend and what Chris would consider to be a friend. He was certainly happy to be Emma's Facebook friend, even if it was one of 400. At least he saw her often which moved it into the real world. Sadly, she had a boyfriend at the time they had met. He was a sporty, athletic type. Not that it would have made much difference had she not as it was unlikely Chris would have had the confidence to ask her out. Girls like Emma did not go out with guys like Chris. Happily, they were no longer together and Emma had said he was not really her type. Chris thought optimistically that maybe he would be her type, reserved, studious and wearing glasses. He could live in hope.

- What engages you so? Emma continued, taking a bit of toast from his plate and bringing him back into the present.
- Oh, hey. Just reading the newspaper, there's been a dead girl found in the park.
- Cheery. I thought you had a lecture this morning?
- Not till 11
- Well it's 10.45 now. Daydreaming again?
- Day dreaming is not permitted in computer programming. What have you got on today?
- A tutorial with Professor Bury on the psychology of serial killers.
- In that case the murder story in the paper should interest you, said Chris getting up to leave.
- Leave the paper and I'll take a look.

Chris left the paper on the table and hurried off with a wave.

Chris had always been interested in computers. It was the generation of software technology. He was 23 and had lived all his life in an era of mobile phones, social media and interactive gaming. It was *The Matrix* in reality. It was now possible to live your entire life without physical interaction with other human beings. And this was supposedly the advancement of mankind. To live your life in computers. To tweet your every thought. He had once stood in Speakers' Corner in Hyde Park and observed the people orating. These people were considered to be at best eccentric and at worst dismissed as loonies by passers-by. And most people did indeed hurry by with barely a glance in their direction. But now via social media every thought could be espoused no matter how trivial. And the thing is, most of them are trivial. Pictures of cups of coffee or frosted cakes with accompanying comments that the writer feels obliged to share with the world. And people ridiculed those at Speakers' Corner!

Chris loved computers. It gave you access to information otherwise unobtainable. At least it did if you understood computers as well as Chris did, if you were as good at software engineering as Chris, if you were one of the top computer hackers in the UK. Not that Chris did anything bad or hacked into anything too sensitive. He knew hackers, good hackers, who had got into trouble by being too inquisitive. National security services did not take kindly to being hacked. Chris did not hack for malicious reasons or personal gain. He did it for the challenge mainly, although he did occasionally earn money from correcting flaws in an organisation's system. You had to tread carefully as IT Heads did not appreciate having their work undermined. Chris was a fairly diplomatic person and generally managed to do it without putting anyone's nose too out of joint. He had spent the summer in America and had earned good money removing a virus for a large national company. But Chris would give up all his computer genius, and he really was a computer genius, to get close to a girl, and one girl in particular, Emma.

So, Chris shared a flat with Liam. It worked well as Liam was very tidy and orderly though he didn't like anyone in his room and always kept in locked. Liam shared his interest in computers and would have made a good computer programmer had he not chosen psychology. In fact, Liam had created several computer programmes and Chris had taken him into his confidence and taught him the basics of hacking. Liam and Chris were fellow gamers in the online fantasy game World of Warcraft set in the fictitious land of Azeroth. Most online "friends" stay that way, never moving into the world of the real. However, Chris and Liam had formed a bond forged in World of Warcraft. Chris had been an Elf wizard for some years gaining much experience of the game. Chris was not overly concerned with being a raw fighter and preferred the subtle magic abilities of a wizard.

Liam was an Elf warrior which struck Chris as being in stark contrast to his actual persona. That was common in the game. You could become the figure you dreamed of being. This usually meant big, strong and muscular with astonishing combat skills. And that was Liam's character, Karlazard the Destroyer. In actuality Liam was small and slight and not particularly athletic. That's the beauty of fantasy. However, this had not stopped Karlazard from being slain by a horde of Orcs. Once dead Karlazard became a phantasm and this is what Avalok, Chris's character, came across and using his magic powers brought back to life. This created a strong connection between the two. After that they always went on quests together. During one of these quests they were joined by Vasika. Vasika was a curvaceous and busty warrior nymph wearing quite revealing battle armour. She had long cascading blonde hair and enchanting eyes. In reality if they met a girl who looked like her in a bar they would be too nervous to talk to her. But on the internet everyone can hide behind a mask. The game also allows for more intimate liaisons and Chris observed that Karlazard and Vasika were heading in this direction. Chris decided to do a bit of hacking on Vasika. It was easy for him to hack into the account on World of Warcraft. He discovered that Vasika was registered to a Ralph Woodman, a bricklayer who lived in Newcastle. He shared this information with Liam. Chris re-collected they had quite a discussion on the topic. Chris started tentatively unsure how Liam would react as there had already been a lot of flirting between Karlazard and Vasika.

- I've been doing some research into some of the characters in World of Warcraft.
- You mean hacking accounts, said Liam who knew Chris all too well.
- Yes, conceded Chris. - One character in particular.
- Vasika? he ventured.

There was no fooling these psychology students.

- That she's really a lumberjack called Hank? continued Liam.
- Ralph, Chris corrected. - A bricklayer from Newcastle.
- Disappointing.

And Liam did indeed look disappointed. It's one thing suspecting the truth, that still leaves room for some hope, quite another to have the truth confirmed which extinguishes any.

Liam had no sexual interest in men, his porn collection was evidence of that. He was definitely attracted to Vasika even though he now had it confirmed it was a man named Ralph. So what was he drawn to? The visual image of a sexy female or the verbal flirtation of a male? If Karlazard interacted sexually with Vasika was this a heterosexual or a homosexual relationship? To what extent was Liam Karlazard or Ralph Vasika? They stopped questing with Vasika.

So, Chris and Liam had met taking their friendship from Azeroth to London. Being at the same university it was easy. They had arranged to meet in the student union bar on campus and found they had a lot in common being similar types of people. Both fairly quiet and studious and with good imaginations and a love of computer technology that drew them into role playing fantasy games. After a few beers they had cemented their friendship.

Chris mused on the word "friend". It really had become bastardised. An online or social media friend could be someone you had never met. Maybe the friend of a friend. Maybe not even that weak reference. How many teenage girls had a Facebook friend called Mandy who was in reality a 50-year-old man with dubious motives? That is the thing about the internet, you can be anyone you want to be. However, Chris was a genuine person and being reasonably comfortable with himself did not create a false online persona. That was at the end of last year. Chris had spent the summer working for a computer company in California and at the start of the new term Liam had found a two-bedroom flat near the university that they could move into. It was in a quiet residential block, ideal for final year study.

Emma got to Professor Bury's room just before 12.00. The room was on the second floor with a large window that over-looked the court. Against the wall was a tall bookcase with four shelves crammed with books and folders. The professor's desk was strewn with papers and half open books. Professor Bury was not in the room but the usual suspects were in their usual positions in the semi-circle of chairs. She noted how people always go to the same spot, we are such creatures of habit. Liam was there, quiet and considered. It's the quiet ones you have to watch for. It's always a mistake to under-estimate the quiet, the less they say the more they are taking in. On the other side of the universe we have Jane Ericsson. If you are not deafened by her voice you will be deafened by her appearance. She calls it seductive but slutty would be a more accurate description. If her skirt was any shorter it would be a belt. And a top worn to expose as much cleavage as possible without being illegal. If she couldn't get a first with perspicacity she would not be averse to achieving, it between her legs. And on that note we come to Will Dumas, God's gift to women in his own mind. A man whose definition of success was how many women he had bedded. Not that he was unattractive being tall, athletic with wavy blonde hair and almost mesmerising eyes. However, Emma's main thought of him was of being a bit of a knob. A self-righteous self-opinionated knob at that.

The knob looked up just as Emma entered.

- Emma, bon jour. And may I say how very demure you look today.

Emma felt like throwing up.

- Hey, she said weakly.

- But I think you would look even more alluring in Jane's skirt, he said lasciviously.
- I'm not sure we'll both fit in Jane's skirt, replied Emma.
- Good point. Jane take it off.
- Fuck off Will, said Jane curtly.
- Very pithy. Not quite the wit of Oscar Wilde. Not that my expectations were high.
- Your last girlfriend said much the same.
- What's the matter Jane, didn't you get any last night? I could help you out there.
- What's the matter Will? No bimbos for you to pick up in the bar last night.
- Touché. Ah, Professor Bury.

The figure of a small, bald man stood in the doorway. His tweed jacket giving away his age. He shuffled to his desk and eased himself into is well-worn chair, evidence of many years spent in study and research.

- So, we continue today with our analysis of the mind of the serial killer. Man has had an innate desire to kill since the dawn of time. Since Cain killed Abel if you subscribe to that particular belief system. The reasons man kills are manifold: love, power, money, revenge. All these can be rationalised, but we are interested in a psyche, infinitely darker, beyond rationale. Killing for the sheer pleasure of killing. The serial killer. But we must try to understand the mind of the serial killer for to recognise the mind of the serial killer is to stop the serial killer. There is a fascination about the serial killer. Even to the point of romanticising him. So, what can we say about him? What drives him?

Professor Bury looked at Will. Will would be the first to speak. Will was always first to speak. A psychological group norm that the professor knew well. Will spoke

- The serial killer derives a drug-like high from killing. Unparalleled pleasure, intrinsically sexual and aggressive against women.
- Not just against women, corrected Emma. - While it is always violent the sexual preference can be homosexuality as in the cases of the American serial killers Jeffrey Dhammer and John Wayne Gacey.
- Quite so Emma, observed Professor Bury. - If today we concentrate on seral killers driven by heterosexual desire can we evaluate the men in terms of their psyche and motivation?
- There is a deep-rooted hatred of women, elaborated Emma. - As in the cases of Peter Sutcliffe, the Yorkshire Ripper and the American Green River Killer, Gary Ridgway.
- That can be largely narrowed down to a hatred of one class of female, added Jane. - Namely prostitutes.
- In part, conceded Emma, - But that does not explain Ted Bundy. The girls he killed were not prostitutes. In fact, mainly they were students.
- Many females are both, said Will cynically.

Jane scowled at him venomously.

Emma was not taking the bait

- Controversial as ever Will.
- I feel we are getting off topic, rebuked Professor Bury. - We are here to analyse the mind of the serial killer not what students do in their spare time.

Will laughed in his supercilious way. The professor's smugness at his idea of a joke exposing a glimpse of his own chauvinism.

Emma continued

- And sexual attack as a driver does not explain Jack the Ripper.
- A weirdo who collected the uteri of the women he slayed, dismissed Jane.
- No. The greatest serial killer of them all.

Everyone looked towards the unknown voice. In the doorway stood a tall slender figure dressed all in black. A long shirt coming down over his jeans which were tucked into pointed black boots that came almost to his knee. His hair was long, black and greasy framing his thin face and pointed beard. He walked slowly into the room picking up a book from the desk and raising a languid eyebrow upon reading the title *Gary Ridgway: Americas Greatest Serial Killer.*

He snorted derisively.

- It certainly isn't Gary Ridgway.
- He killed the most, said Jane dismissing this odd-looking guy. No-one looking that odd could have anything intelligent to say. - Ergo he is the greatest.
- He had a fatal flaw, said the stranger, amused.
- Which was?
- He got caught.

Professor Bury roared with laughter.

- Allow me to introduce our expert on Jack the Ripper, Patrick Blackburn. Patrick is here on a sabbatical from the University of Los Angeles doing research. Perhaps we could arrange a tutorial with our budding psychologists.

Patrick looked around the students somewhat sceptically then smiled unnervingly, placing the book on the desk.

- Tomorrow afternoon, 2pm, in my room, he said decisively

He turned on his heels and disappeared through the doorway.

Chapter 2

Liam was sat in the living room when Chris returned to the flat. The room was sparsely furnished with a small, worn sofa facing the television and an old armchair beside it. There was a low, glass-topped table in front of the sofa which Liam had covered in notes from the tutorial earlier. Chris looked over his shoulder.

- It must be interesting studying the mind of the serial killer, he observed.
- Not without interest, replied Liam. - We were introduced to an interesting character today.
- Oh yes, said Chris with raised eyebrows.
- Yea, an odd type. American. Apparently, he specialises in Jack the Ripper. Dresses like he could have been around in 19th century Whitechapel.
- Where was he in the early hours of the morning? asked Chris mischievously.
- Early hours of the morning?
- Was he near Regent's Park?
- Regent's Park?
- Don't you read the newspapers?
- Well not today. What's the story?
- A girl was found murdered.
- Let me see your paper.
- I gave it to Emma.
- Oh, Emma, said Liam knowingly.
- Did you see her today?
- Yes, she was in Professor Bury's tutorial.

Chris said nothing. He went into the kitchen, picked up the kettle and took it to the sink to fill it with water. Liam watched him carefully from the sofa. Chris remained silent as he switched the kettle on and returned to the living room.

- I don't think she is seeing anyone at present, offered Liam.

Chris stayed silent.

- Why don't you ask her out?
- I don't know. It seems harder now that we have become friends.
- I think it would be harder if you were complete strangers.
- Yes, maybe, but there seems to be more to lose now. It could make our friendship awkward.
- I overheard her talking with Jane Ericsson. She is working at that bar tonight, "Monte Carlo". You could always pop in.
- Monte Carlo? I don't think so. It's over-priced and pretentious.
- World of Warcraft then?

Monday night at Bar Monte Carlo was quiet. It was supposedly an upmarket wine bar. That meant mainly expensive. Keep the riff raff out. Of course that depends on your definition of riffraff. The bar owner was what is popularly called "a bit of a character". He was in his late 40s and believed himself to have, "a fantastic body, better than most men half my age", to use his own words. It is true he did go regularly to the gym where he apparently only worked on his chest and arms. Judging by his bulging belly he did most of his work on that in the bar. He was permanently tanned, or better said oranged, with a style that was fashionable 30 years ago. Who in this day and age had a dyed blonde mullet and wore white trousers with a Hawaiian shirt? Keith Hammond, that's who. A legend in his own mind. Married but open to offers, especially when he was making the offers, and he made plenty of them.

Keith was leaning on the bar chatting to a couple of the regulars who Emma knew to be called Smithy and Gatesy. The thought that had gone into these nicknames really was quite breath-taking. Imagine calling a man whose surname was Smith "Smithy". The creative juices were really flowing there. Though why you would give a man in his 40s a nickname never ceased to amaze Emma. Of course she knew it was all to do with male social bonding. The first time she heard Smithy call Keith "Hammy" she had to rush down to the cellar and laughed her socks off. Laughing in his face would probably be deemed rude and possibly insubordinate. You always had to respect position if not the person. Emma was working with Lisa tonight. At 19 years old she was a few years younger than Emma. Lisa had worked at Bar Monte Carlo since leaving school. She was a small, slim girl with shoulder length blonde hair and undeniably pretty which drew a lot of male attention. Unfortunately, from Emma's perspective, some of this attention had come from Will Dumas and she was now infatuated with the colossal prick. Obviously, Bar Monte Carlo was the kind of place that attracted Will Dumas and his like. Emma had tried to dissuade Lisa from going out with him but he managed to work his dubious charms and now they were "very much in love". Well, she was.

Emma tried to avoid drawing the attention of Keith and co. Too late.

- Ah, talk of the devil, alerted Keith.

Damn, they had obviously been talking about her, that was unsettling for a start off.

- Any sign of a boyfriend yet? asked Keith.

What do you say to personal questions like that? Fuck off and mind your own business was Emma's first thought.

- Too busy studying and working for boyfriends. *Pathetic. Should have gone with fuck off.*
- Perhaps she would prefer an older man, leered Smithy amusing the others.

Have you looked in the mirror you fat balding twat?

She smiled weakly. Could she be any more pathetic?

Keith put his arm around her waist.

- What you need is an experienced man of the world, he purred.

Emma was cringing inside. She had a sneaking admiration for women who could tell a guy to fuck off but there were not many of them. So you had to put up with it.

- I'd better get to work Keith, she said wriggling free from his hand which was getting lower.
- She's a good girl, said Keith to his gang giving her a last squeeze. - Lisa is down in the cellar getting stock, go and give her a hand"
- I'll give her a hand, piled on Gatesy.

Emma headed swiftly off with their lecherous laughter ringing in her ears. The cellar door was beside the bar. She opened the door and was relieved to find the light at the top of the stairs working. It was always at best 50-50 whether it would work. Keith said it was faulty electrics but had not bothered to get it fixed. Anyway, tonight Emma was able to make her way down without risking breaking her neck. At the bottom it was filled with metal beer barrels, crates of lager bottles and boxes of spirits. She found Lisa kneeling down assembling bottles. There was a black cat rubbing its body against her thighs. She reached down and gently stroked it behind the ear causing it to purr.

- You're so cute, Suki. What are you doing down here?
- Probably hiding from Keith, you know how fond he is of pussy.
- Oh, Em, you're terrible, she said looking up and giggling.

Lisa Conway was easy to get along with. Undemanding and inoffensive. There was quite an innocence about her.

- Hey, Lisa. Are you hiding down here from Keith and his cronies?
- They are in a good mood this evening. Apparently, Keith got a tip and they all won money on some horse race.
- That explains the pawing I got almost as soon as I walked through the door. Jesus, no doubt it will be worse later after a few drinks. Better keep busy and out of their way.

Lisa laughed her sweet laugh. Emma knew there was no way she was going to tell anyone to fuck off. Although Lisa did have the advantage that when Will was in the bar Keith and gang left her alone. They knew Will and gave him respect, from what Emma could gather, because he was good at football. Being good at football got you some kind of knighthood at Bar Monte Carlo. However, this security for Lisa meant double potential trouble for Emma as they emerged from the cellar. And there he is with Keith. Bollocks, thought Emma.

Will was being his usual loud self. He seemed to be pontificating on the usual topic, football. Emma knew this because she heard "Feyenoord" mentioned and while having no real interest in football herself she knew this to be a football team. Holland or possibly Belgium.

She remembered one night when Liam and Chris were in the bar, not that they came in very often. Emma knew it was not really their kind of place. It was the first time she had met Chris. Liam had introduced them. Chris struck Emma as being quite reserved though he had greeted her with a warm, genuine smile. They had sat with Keith and Will who were heatedly discussing the last game that their team had lost.

- Terrible refereeing again, said Keith shaking his head with the apparent trauma of it all.

Emma knew it to be a universal law of football that if your team lost it was always the referee's fault. Nothing to do with tactics or that the other team were better.

- That was never a penalty, continued Keith in despair.
- The defender did make contact with him in the penalty area, joined in Chris.
- Yes, said Keith. - But not hard enough to be a foul.
- So you can make contact with another player in the box? queried Emma.

- It wasn't hard enough for him to bring the player down, defended Keith.
- Did he get brought down? continued Emma.
- Yes, conceded Keith, - but he made a meal of it.
- The rules all seem very vague, concluded Emma.
- I think the game is unrefereeable, concluded Chris.
- How so? asked Emma.
- Well, you only have four officials covering 22 players and a playing area of approximately 100 by 70 metres. If you contrast this with tennis an area 10 times less than a football pitch, and 2 or 4 players. At a top Grand Slam tournament, like, Wimbledon will be 10 officials on centre court.
- That's a completely different sport, said an increasingly exasperated Keith.
- Ok, let's take American football, said Chris taking a different tack. - A similar size of playing area but that has 7 officials and they use video technology for all contentious decisions.

Keith threw his arms into the air.

- And their rules are much clearer, continued Chris undeterred.
- You don't understand football, said Will who had been listening with a condescending smile on his face. - You don't play the game. Furthermore, it's only nerds over here that watch American football. Guys who aren't any good at real football".

Keith laughed. Chris had nothing to say to that disparaging remark. It was true he wasn't good at football. He knew Will's type. Guys who were good and used this to undermine the opinions of others. Emma on the other hand had been quite impressed with Chris's reasoned argument.

That was some time ago but sometimes life felt like Groundhog Day. The same people in the same places and having the same conversations. Lisa saw Will. Her face lit up and she went over to him.

- There's my girl, said Will putting his arm around her and giving her arse a little squeeze.
- Stop, protested Lisa pulling away with an embarrassed giggle.
- You're a lucky guy, said Keith who would love to get his hands on Lisa's nubile body.
- I've got to work, said Lisa giving him a kiss as she headed off to the other end of the bar.
- You're the fortunate one, being surrounded all day by hot chicks, replied Will while casting his eye over a red head who was sitting at a table opposite.
- Owning the bar has its advantages, said Keith with a knowing grin.

The red head looked up catching Will's gaze. Will gave her his cheeky smile. She smiled back then turned hurriedly back to her friends.

- I haven't seen her before, said Will.
- That's Marie, replied Keith. - Been coming in the past few Friday's with the leggy blonde.
- Maybe I'll pop in this Friday, said Will.
- I thought you might, laughed Keith patting him on the back. - You're a man after my own heart. Why have one girl when you can have them all?

The rest of the evening passed uneventfully. By the end of the night Emma was ready to go home. She was with Lisa in the small staffroom.

- Em, I meant to say to you, I'm going to the Falcon for a few drinks with my friend Tina on Friday. Would you like to come?
- Tina? Is that the one with the little girl?
- Yea, she doesn't get out much because she has to look after Jenny.
- Sure. Be good to get away from work and study for a night.
- Great, said Lisa with genuine delight. - I've told Tina all about you.

She gave Emma a hug and they left together.

Chapter 3

Chris did not have any lectures this morning but he was still up at 8.30am. He had heard Liam moving about and the flat door closing as he departed. He got up and went into the kitchen in the t-shirt and boxers he slept in. Hallelujah, there was milk in the fridge. He poured a bowl of cereals, returned to the living room and turned on the television. The news was on, here was an update on the Regent's Park murder.

In the early hours of yesterday morning the body of a young woman was discovered in Regent's Park. The woman has been identified as Penny Holland, a 21-year-old Medical student at University College of London. It is understood she was attacked with a knife near Bayswater Road. The police have cordoned off the area and asked for anyone who was in Regent's Park or the Bayswater Road area to contact them. In other news....

Bloody hell, that murdered girl went to his university. He did not know her, there were too many students, but the closeness made it all too real. Regent's Park was near the university - he had walked through it many times. The story intrigued him, he would like to know more. He decided a bit of hacking was required. Finishing his cereal, he put the bowl in the sink to soak. This would ensure the job of cleaning it later would be easier. Chris was a very pragmatic and efficient person. He went to his room, turned his computer on and started to hack the local newspaper. He had hacked it before so knew how to get access. The lead journalist on the murder story was Dave Preston. Hacking his emails would be a good place to start.

This guy, Dave, certainly had a lot of emails. Follow up on an assault in Piccadilly, squash with Greg on Thursday, new story on possible arson in Stepney, sexist joke from someone called Paul. Ah, email from Inspector John Parnell, London Metropolitan Police. This looked more promising:

Email from John Parnell to Dave Preston

Dave, what we were speaking about this morning, I still can't give clearance to print any details of the exact nature of the wounds at present. We do not want to sensationalise the nature of this already horrific attack.

Horrific attack? What did that mean? Chris was becoming more interested in this story by the minute. Nothing else of interest in the emails of Dave Preston. He would need to hack this Inspector Parnell at the Met if he wanted to know more. That would be more difficult but by no means impossible. It would also take Chris onto more perilous ground. The police did not take kindly to being hacked. Chris decided to do nothing at present though there was something more sinister in this story. He turned off his computer and went for a shower.

Emma was the first to arrive at Patrick's room. The door was open; she could see Patrick silhouetted against the window. Emma entered the room and sat in one of the chairs that was arranged in a semi-circle in front of the desk. He barely looked up. The room was quite small. His desk was untidy, covered in books, some open, some closed. There were a few black and white photos half exposed below the books. One was of a corpse of a woman lying on a mortuary table. It looked like she had an autopsy as the torso was cut from the throat to the naval. The picture beside it was a woman dressed in ragged untidy clothes but wearing a new black straw bonnet. Emma recognised her as Mary Ann Nichols, better known as Polly Nichols, the first murder victim of Jack the Ripper. Patrick observed Emma as she studied the photos.

- Polly Nichols, said Patrick. - The first murder victim of Jack the Ripper.

Emma looked up. His penetrating eyes were fixed on her.

- She was an alcoholic and prostitute. She had been married but her husband, William Nichols, tired of her immoral ways, separated from her. Destitute, she was forced to go to Lambeth Workhouse where she lived on and off before finally lodging in a doss house in Spitalfields named Wilmott's. She sold her body for the measly sum of 3 pence, the price of a glass of gin.

His dark penetrating eyes never faltered from Emma's as he spoke, carefully analysing her every reaction. Emma remained silent. Patrick continued.

- It was Thursday 30th August 1888. Polly Nichols went to Whitechapel to solicit. It was past midnight when she returned to the doss house. She was drunk having spent any money she earned on gin. Although she was wearing a new straw bonnet. It was small and black trimmed with black velvet. Having no money, she was thrown out. She went back to Whitechapel and was never seen alive again. Her bloodied body was discovered in Buck's Row. The throat was cut from ear to ear and several stab wounds to the abdomen.

Patrick paused and waited for Emma's thoughts.

- It was a terrible indictment of Victorian Britain that women were forced to live this way, proclaimed Emma.
- Has anything really changed? contested Patrick. - We still have prostitution and we still have destitution.
- We don't have Dickensian workhouses.
- We do still have serial killers, said Patrick changing tack. - There was the Regent's Park killing.
- That isn't part of a series, said Emma mildly shocked by this statement.
- Isn't it?
- Nothing has been said to that effect in the news.
- Not everything that occurs is made known, said Patrick mysteriously.

Emma was slightly perplexed.

- There is nothing to suggest it is part of a series.

Patrick continued.

- Every serial killer starts with one killing. The series is not apparent until there are more.

Emma looked at Patrick perplexed. She was just about to speak when the other students arrived. What was Patrick referring to? What did he know?

When Chris got back to the flat that night it was late. He could hear Liam in his room. Chris only had one thing on his mind, the murder of the college girl in Regent's Park. He was inquisitive by nature, that was the main reason he loved to hack. He revelled in knowing what other people did not. All day he had mulled over whether to hack the police report. It was certainly illegal and there was a high degree of danger but that only made it more appealing to Chris. He backed away from potential physical danger. As a teenager he had declined to do a bungee jump for charity. The danger of plunging to your death seemed all too real. However, sat in the safe familiarity of your bedroom any danger seemed distant, almost non-existent. It's only when you receive a loud banging on your front door in the early hours of the morning from the police that the full extent of the risk becomes apparent. It must be quite a shock for people. Despite knowing all this Chris decided he was going to hack the Met.

He set his computer up and loaded the code breaking software he had designed himself. It would take a while to run. He brought up the Metropolitan Police site and started the code breaking programme. While the combinations permutated he went into the kitchen to make tea and something to eat. Hopefully, it would not take too long. He had hacked into the university system previously. That had taken less than an hour. He actually felt a bit bad because he had used it to check out Liam. His middle name was Tarquin. Tarquin. That had made Chris laugh. Rather too posh a name for the son of a lorry driver and a nurse living in a small mid-terrace house in a former welsh mining village. He bet the name Tarquin went down well at the local school.

The programme was still running when Chris returned to his room. He got his daily folder out and sorted through his notes from the day's lectures. There were folders for each subject, colour coded and filed alphabetically on the top row of his bookshelf above his textbooks which were also in alphabetical order. He did the same with his extensive DVD collection. People had criticised Chris for doing this suggesting he had a compulsive disorder. Chris had countered that logic was the reason for alphabetical ordering. He wanted to spend his evening watching a film not looking for it. Chris loved logic but he often wondered if some people simply did not get it. Chris's thoughts were interrupted by a sudden buzzing. He looked at his computer. He was in.

Sitting at his desk he scanned for Inspector John Parnell. Eventually he found his name. He now had access to all his reports and emails. It would be a file created yesterday or today. His eyes scanned the list fervently. There it was "Holland, Penny". Chris manoeuvred his icon over the file with his mouse and clicked. The file opened. Chris read:

Holland, Penny

The mutilated body was discovered in Regent's Park 3:15am Monday 18 October 2016 by a Gerald Hopper who was walking his dog. He alerted the police via his mobile phone. Homicide, myself included and forensics were called to the crime scene arriving at 4:00am. Examination of the cadaver revealed the throat had been cut from ear to ear with a large sharp knife. Additionally, there were 9 stab wounds to the abdomen made in all probability with the same knife. These stab wounds seem to have been done in a frenzied attack after the initial throat cutting. Case of homicide by person unknown.

The girl was wearing a blue denim jacket, white blouse, black mini-skirt, black stockings and black high-heeled stiletto shoes. She had a white handbag which contained make-up, white knickers and £500 in used £10 and £20 notes. There was evidence of sexual activity but not forced and it did not occur at the crime scene. My conclusion is that she was working as a prostitute and operating out of premises. At present location unknown.

Emma had spent the rest of the day after her meeting with Patrick in the library. The way he had spoken about Jack the Ripper was unnerving. He almost had an admiration for him.

It was late when she got back to her flat. Habitually she turned on her computer and went straight to Facebook. Photo from mum of dad's birthday. Astonished as she was that her mum had been able to upload a photo. There they were wearing hats and a picture of a cake. Then a message from Jane.

I heard Lisa is having a night out at the Falcon Friday. Might come along.

You had to admire the woman's gall inviting herself. Emma supposed it would be alright though, Jane was often in Bar Monte Carlo and Lisa knew her. She sent Lisa a message about Jane wanting to come to the night out. As she guessed Lisa was on Facebook and in her typical friendly way was happy for Jane to come. Emma fired off a message to Jane with arrangements for Friday. She turned the computer off and got ready for bed.

Chapter 4

Emma went to Chris and Liam's flat the following morning. She pressed the intercom. After a while she heard Chris's voice.

- Hello.
- Hi. It's Emma.

Chris had only just woken up. Emma's voice immediately brought him to life.

- Hey. Come up. He pressed the door release and heard it click open.

A few moments later Emma was in the flat, Chris showed her into the sitting room. Her auburn hair seemed to shine with life and her eyes sparkled. Then again that was the way Chris always seemed to see Emma. He hoped his distant adoration of her was not showing although he had read somewhere that a girl always knows.

- I'd love a tea Chris, said Emma smiling and breaking his delicious fantasy.

Yep a girl always knows.

- Of course, replied Chris heading for the kitchen. - Milk no sugar, right?
- That's right, I'm sweet enough, said Emma teasingly.

A girl definitely always knows.

Should Chris make a response?

You certainly are. Too obvious.

You're the sweetest girl I know. Too over the top.

In the end Chris said nothing. At least he hadn't said anything awkward.

He returned with the teas and sat down in the armchair adjacent to Emma.

- Is Liam still in bed?
- No. He's left already.
- God, said Emma with mild irritation. - We arranged to meet here this morning to go over our research.

Chris took a sip from his cup. Emma had a look of annoyance on her pretty face. Chris could feel the mood changing for the worse. He had to break that.

- So, what's new with you? he asked.

No reply. Had she heard him. Her brow was furrowed with growing ire.

- What's new with you? risked Chris again smiling hoping to get her light mood back.

She looked up, sighed then smiled.

- Oh, not much although I did have an interesting encounter with the new research graduate from America, said Emma taking a sip from her cup.
- Liam mentioned meeting him.
- His name is Patrick Blackburn.
- Liam said he is a bit odd, specialises in Jack the Ripper.
- Yea he's pretty weird. Dresses in black with long greasy hair.

- Sounds a bit like a goth, joked Chris

Emma put her tea down. Her bright face became more sombre.

- It's more than just the look. There's something about him, something unnerving. His eyes seem to penetrate you when he looks at you.
- Probably just an act, offered Chris.
- No. There was a dark aura about his room. A cold that almost touched you. He had photos of the mutilated body of Polly Nichols.
- Who's Polly Nichols?
- She was the first murder victim of Jack the Ripper.
- What was the picture like? probed Chris.
- Horrific. Her throat was cut from ear to ear and she had multiple stab wounds to her body.

Chris sat up on the edge of his chair, his eyes suddenly alert.

- Where on the body were these stab wounds?
- In the abdomen.

Chris's mind was now fully focused.

- How many stab wounds?

Emma was puzzled by Chris's eagerness for these details.

- About 10, I guess.

Chris slumped back in the armchair and let out a sharp exhalation of breath.

- Uncanny, he muttered.
- What is It? asked Emma becoming increasingly concerned.

Chris was silent his mind working overtime.

- Chris, said Emma leaning towards him and nudging him. - What is it?

Chris looked at her.

- The girl who was killed in Regent's Park had the exact same wounds.

Emma looked puzzled.

- How do you know that? I never heard that in the news.
- No, it's not been made public.
- Then how do you know?

Chris looked at Emma. This was decision time. He did not make it widely known he was a computer hacker. The less people that knew the safer for him. He looked at her imploring eyes, her beautiful imploring eyes. He made his decision.

- I'll show you.

He got up and walked toward the door beckoning Emma to follow. They went into Chris's room. He sat in front of his desk and turned the computer on. Emma stood behind him somewhat perplexed as the computer came to life. Chris went to his files, a document opened.

- Metropolitan police? said Emma quizzically.

Chris got up.

- Sit here, he said offering his chair to Emma. - You can read it for yourself.

Emma sat in front of the computer and read the police report on Penny Holland. Chris sat on the edge of his bed and waited anxiously for Emma's response.

- This is incredible, said Emma finally. - These wounds mirror exactly those of Polly Nichols.
- Could be a coincidence, said Chris though it was clear he did not believe this.
- And the police believe this girl was a prostitute?
- So it seems. It would account for the way she was dressed and having all that money on her,
- The same as Polly Nichols?
- Apparently.
- And someone has arrived in London with a fixation on Jack the Ripper. We have to go to the police with this, said Emma decisively.
- Hold on there, said Chris suddenly startled. - And say what?
- That this is a copy-cat Jack the Ripper murder and we know who did it.
- We don't know who did it, said Chris hurriedly. - All we know is that there are certain parallels with the killings and that someone specialises in Jack the Ripper.
- The police can at least investigate, protested Emma.
- The only person the police will investigate is me for hacking, said Chris. - I'll be sent down for two years. And what about you? That sort of slanderous talk is going to affect your graduation prospects.

Emma could see his point. She was not a hysterical person and quickly put things into perspective.

- I suppose you're right, she conceded. – We should do something though.
- We could do some investigating of our own ventured Chris.
- Like what?
- We could find out more about this girl Penny Holland.
- How?
- I could hack into her accounts, emails, Facebook, university record.
- Ok. Let's try her Facebook page. Find out who her friends were. Find out what she was like.

Chris sat in front of the computer and pulled up Penny's Facebook page. Last entry 17 October. Day before she died. More pictures of bloody coffee cups and cakes observed Chris. He scrolled down. Nothing of interest. More scrolling. Holiday photos. More coffee cups and cakes. Scrolling down, scrolling down.

- STOP, shouted Emma looking at a photo that had just appeared on the screen.

Chris stopped scrolling. The picture seemed to be taken at a party. There were four women in fancy dress standing together in a dimly lit room. Judging from the clothes it was period dress from the end of the 19th century. The girl on the right was wearing a brown bodice with a long black skirt. She was holding a purple fan in front of her face. The girl beside her wore a white blouse and dark green skirt and had a cream shawl over her head. On the left of the photo a girl had a black cloth jacket over a white blouse and long red skirt below which were black lace up boots. She had a red neckerchief but her face was also obscured by a black fan. The girl beside her was wearing a rust coloured ulster, a brown frock down to the floor and a black bonnet.

- Can you enlarge the photo? asked Emma

Chris enlarged the photo.

- Focus on the girl in the hat.

Chris brought the girl in the hat in to focus.

- That's Penny Holland, observed Chris.
- There's more, added Emma. – I've seen that hat before. It's the same as Polly Nichol's bonnet.
- Why don't you ask Professor Bury about the Ripper murders?
- Ok. I'll ask him tomorrow, replied Emma getting up to go.
- Wait, said Chris staring at the screen. – There's something else. A title below the picture.

Emma leant forward and read the title – The Ripper Club.

- What does this mean? wondered Emma with concern.
- Jack the Ripper?

Chris escorted Emma to the door. As Emma walked down the stairs from the flat she could not help but feel a certain disquiet that this was only the beginning of something sinister.

That evening Emma was back in Bar Monte Carlo. The usual suspects were at the bar, Hammy, Gatesy, Smithy and Will. Doing their usual, appraising girls in their lascivious manner. They all fancied themselves as players, despite their age and appearance. In the case of Will, Emma knew this to be true and with Lisa not working tonight he was scanning his prey like a hawk ready to swoop. Emma watched as he sidled over to a red head sat alone in a booth. She seemed to re-collect that Keith had said her name was Marie McCarthy. Emma didn't know much about her. Will really was a piece of work, using his wily charms, which judging by the giggling was working. Emma busied herself about the bar.

Sometime later she had to go to the cellar to re-stock. She was alone in the basement although she could faintly hear the rancour above in the bar. Suddenly she felt arms around her waist.

- Keith stop, she said wriggling free.

She turned and was shocked to find herself face to face with Will.

- What are you doing down here? she demanded.
- I came to be with you, he replied reaching forward for her.

She pushed him away

- You're disgusting. Do you think girls will just fall at your feet? I don't know what Lisa sees in you. She deserves better."

Will's manner changed dramatically.

- You little bitch. You're going to get what's coming to you.
- Get out! screamed Emma.
- I'm going you cheap slut, he hissed turning and heading up the stairs.

Emma was shaking and tears were beginning to well in her eyes. Bastard. But what could she do? Will and Keith were as thick as thieves. She hated this fucking place. She would have left a long time ago but she needed the money to finish her studies. Just six more months and she would be out of this sexist hellhole she told herself. She tidied herself up and went back up to the bar. To her relief Will was leaving with Marie. She felt sorry for Lisa but relieved he was going. She wanted to tell everything to Lisa but what good would that do. Lisa worshipped the ground he should be trodden into. To tell her would only damage their friendship. She would never believe Emma. Love really is blind. Best to say nothing. She was having a girls' night out tomorrow. A good drink would get her mind off things. Drink, the cause of and answer to all of life's problems.

The following morning she was back in Professor Bury's room for another tutorial. Emma steeled herself, she did not want to draw attention to the fact that she was looking for information on Patrick.

- Professor could you tell us about Jack the Ripper.
- Certainly, but Patrick could tell you more.
- I only wanted a brief outline.
- Very well

He started

- Jack the Ripper was a serial killer in London at the end of the 19th century. The exact number of murders committed by him is the subject of considerable debate. It is widely believed there were only 5 killings, collectively known as the canonical 5: Polly Nichols,

Annie Chapman, Elizabeth Stride, Catherine Eddowes and Mary Kelly. All the murders took place at the end of 1888. There are various theories as to who Jack the Ripper really was but his identity remains a mystery. The bodies were all mutilated with body parts being removed. It is believed the killer had some medical knowledge to perform these crude dissections.

- What happened to the belongings of the victims? ventured Emma.
- Well after the police had finished examining them, I imagine they would be taken by the families of the victims.

Of course, thought Emma, the families.

Chapter 5

Emma got to The Falcon at 8 o'clock. The Falcon was an easy unpretentious bar frequented by young twenty somethings, young workers and students alike. There was always a good lively atmosphere helped by the reasonable price of the drinks. The place was mobbed as usual and Emma had to weave her way through the mass of bodies looking for Lisa and her friend.

- Em!

She heard Lisa calling and then saw her waving enthusiastically through the crowd from a little niche.

- Over here!

Emma smiled in acknowledgement and fought her way to the niche. Lisa got up and kissed Emma on both cheeks. We are very European these days.

- This is my friend Tina, said Lisa introducing her friend.

Tina stood up and gave Emma the same European style kisses as Lisa.

- We have champagne, announced Lisa excitedly. - To celebrate Tina's birthday.
- Oh, happy birthday, exclaimed Emma.
- Thank you, replied Tina. - It's hard to get out with Jenny keeping me occupied 24/7. I'm really looking forward to tonight.
- I love your rings, said Emma observing three old fashioned brass rings on her fingers.

- Thanks, replied Tina – they belonged to my grand-mother.

Tina Stanley had been an ordinary girl at an inner London comprehensive school. Her hair was long and thick and a lovely chestnut colour. At school she was popular and had many friends. She played netball for the team and dreamed of becoming a journalist. At 16 she became pregnant and her life changed forever. Some of her friends thought it would be better to have an abortion. Tina struggled with the decision as long as she could and 9 months later gave birth to a beautiful baby girl who she named Jenny, after her grandmother. The father was a boy from her class who was far too immature to deal with the reality of a new-born baby and the responsibilities that brings. Tina did try to make things work as best she could but eventually decided it would be best to do it without him. She got herself a council flat.

- That seems tough, observed Emma. - How do you manage for money?

Lisa looked embarrassed.

- You shouldn't ask things like that Em.
- It's ok, said Tina understandingly. - I'm a cam girl.
- A what? spluttered Emma not sure she had heard properly.
- A cam girl.

Emma was intrigued but not sure how to proceed.

- It's good money and I can work from home, added Tina sensing Emma's uneasiness.

Emma was surprised but impressed with her openness and self-reliance. Tina seemed quite relaxed and willing to talk about it so Emma pressed on.

- What does that involve?
- Well, basically, I have a computer and a web cam. Guys contact me via the website and I earn more money the longer they stay on. You learn quickly who the time wasters are. The key is to get the real clients into your private chatroom.
- How do you do that?
- Well, you have to be seductive but not give too much away in the open chatroom. I usually wear stockings and suspenders, sexy knickers and a blouse. Undoing a few blouse buttons provocatively usually entices someone into a private chat. It's a mistake to show too much. Plenty of guys want a free thrill.
- What happens in the private chatroom? enquired Emma.
- Whatever the client wants. The goal is to keep them chatting as long as you can and to keep them coming back. I have a few regulars, which is good.
- Isn't it dangerous?
- Not really, I use the name Roxanne. No-one knows who I am or where I live. I avoid real weirdos who are into extreme stuff.

Emma was astonished but genuinely interested. Tina was wearing expensive designer clothing which suggested it paid better than Bar Monte Carlo. She was just musing on what you would need to look like to be a cam girl when she got a first-hand experience.

- Champagne! Just what I want.

Jane had arrived. Short tight skirt that barely covered her bum and blouse exposing too much of her ample cleavage. Emma noticed a group of young men ogling Jane from the bar. Which, of course, was exactly the attention Jane wanted. Emma thought this would be the ideal attire for a cam girl.

Chris came in late and went to his room. His mind was occupied with the murder of Penny Holland and its eerie parallels with Polly Nichols. It was certainly strange. Perhaps merely a coincidence. Then there was Patrick Blackburn and his sudden appearance and obsession with Jack the Ripper. These could be deep waters.

Chris was distracted by the front door opening. He glanced at his watch, almost midnight, quite late for Liam to be out. He heard Liam's footsteps crossing the hall and then the door of his room opening and closing followed by the key turning in the lock.

The Falcon was getting busier and the girls had moved on to cocktails. Tina's cam-girl revelation was still the theme of the evening.

- You should consider it Emma, suggested Tina.
- I think it's disgusting, blurted out Jane before Emma could reply. - Old men sat in front of their computers with their pants around their ankles getting off on the erotic display of tarts.

This was an astonishing statement from The Queen of the One Night Stands. Sexual morality is clearly a subjective issue.

There was an awkward silence.

- I'm going to get some crisps, said Jane teetering towards the bar as a result of trying to walk in stilettos after too much to drink
- Ignore her, said Emma breaking the silence. - She's just drunk.

Emma knew it was not because Jane was drunk but she liked Tina and wanted to demonstrate her support.

- I've met her type before, replied Tina thoughtfully. - They appeal to a hypocritical Victorian morality. The way she is dressed she certainly does not intend to be going home alone.

Emma stayed silent. She thought the same.

- Seriously Emma you should consider it. Better money than Bar Monte Carlo.

Emma's attention was on Jane stood at the bar. A young guy in designer clothes and clearly drunk was talking to her. Emma had noticed him earlier in the evening. He seemed to be going around every available woman in the place. Emma had been standing at the bar earlier. This guy had approached the girl beside her and she had overheard the conversation.

- Hey, I think you're gorgeous. Do you want to come back to my place?

That was it. Opening gambit and punchline rolled into one. Could he make any less effort? Emma thought what girl is possibly going to be interested in that minimalist approach. No "Hi what's your name?", no attempt to get to know anything about the girl. He might as well have said "I'm looking for sex but don't want to pay a prostitute".

Emma didn't have to wait long for her answer as Jane left the bar with this guy. Clearly Jane thought being an unpaid prostitute was morally nobler than being a cam girl.

It was late when Patrick got back to his room at the university. He entered without turning on the light. The moonlight shone dimly through the uncovered window. Patrick moved towards the desk and turned on the lamp. He then closed the curtains leaving the desk illuminated but the rest of the room in darkness. He picked up the open file on his desk and started reading.

Annie Chapman

Born September 1841.

5 ft. tall, blue eyes, dark brown wavy hair

Married John Chapman 1 May 1869 (she would have been 28 at the time)

3 children: Emily, Annie and John

Separated 1884. Police report cites reason as her drunken and immoral ways.

During 1886 lived with John Sivvey at 30 Dorset Street, Whitechapel

After they split she took a bed at a lodging House named Crossingham's at 35 Dorset Street. The Lodging House accommodated approximately 300 people.

Saturday 8 September 1888

Just past midnight Annie has an altercation with the night watchman at Crossingham's, John Evans.

- You drunk again Annie?
- What of it if I am? What business is that of yours John Evans?
- Ain't none of my business Annie. Money for your bed, that's my business. Now let's be 'aving it.
- I ain't got it 'ave I.
- Well you better be getting it ain't ya.
- Ah go on ya old git.
- Less 'n you'd rather kip in the gutter.
- I'll get ya money. Don' let me bed. I won' be long before I'm back.

Annie picks up 3 brass rings and puts them on.

- They be new ain't they?
- Lovely ain't they but you ain't 'aving 'em.

Annie staggers out of the lodging house. She makes her way down to Hanbury Street where she meets a man. This is the last time Annie is seen alive. Just before 6am her body is discovered. Her throat was severed deeply with a jagged cut right around her neck. The abdomen was completely laid open and the uterus, vagina and bladder removed. There was an abrasion over the ring finger with distinct markings of rings. No rings were found.

Until now.

Chapter 6

By the time Tina got back it was almost 1am. She had enjoyed the night and had spent a lot of money, mainly on champagne, and was a little drunk. She decided to do bit of caming for an hour or so to make some money back. She slipped out of her dress and peeled black stockings up her shapely legs. Carefully she attached them to her suspender belt ensuring she didn't tear a hole being a bit tipsy. In her draw she found a red G-string and put it on. She slipped on a white blouse leaving the top three buttons undone to give a tantalising glimpse of her cleavage. Sitting down at her computer she lined up the webcam and logged into her camgirl account. She lay back on her bed and waited. She knew it would not be long. Sure enough, the men came like sharks around their prey.

Big john: Hi babe

Steve007: Want to chat honey?

Lord Dong: Take your blouse off

King Kong: Do you wanna see my cock babe?

Suddenly one of the men had entered Tina's private chatroom.

Roxanne: Hi honey. What's your name?

No reply

Perhaps he was shy or nervous. A surprising number of men are.

Roxanne: What would you like?

No reply

Tina wasn't bothered. The clock was running which meant she was earning.

Roxanne: Shall I strip for you?

No reply

Tina started moving erotically, wiggling her hips, pouting, playing provocatively with her long luxurious hair.

Tina's eye caught a message that had suddenly appeared on her screen

JACK1888: I know who you are

Tina was a little unnerved but kept gyrating.

Another message

JACK1888: I know where you live

Tina stopped her act and sat down in front of her computer. Another weirdo.

Roxanne: What's your name?

No reply.

This jerk was annoying Tina with his stupid games.

Roxanne: Who are you?

No reply

Fine. Tina would just sit there and let the clock eat all this dumb fuck's money. Five minutes had already elapsed.

Ten minutes. This was easy money. Suddenly a message appeared.

JACK1888: You're just a cheap whore, aren't you Tina?

Who the fuck was this that knew her name? Maybe he really did know her. Tina was freaked out.

Roxanne: Who the fuck are you?

No reply.

Time to get rid of this jerk. Tina was just about to close the chat when another message appeared.

JACK1888: Does Jenny know what a slut her mother is?

Tina exploded.

Roxanne: Fuck you. You sad little wanker.

She slammed her finger on the close chat button and her screen went blank. That was enough for tonight. She went to bed refusing to allow that prick to ruin her birthday. As she fell asleep the harrowing messages were still going through her mind.

In another part of the city Will entered the block and went up the stairs to the second floor. He walked to the end of the corridor and knocked on the door. It was opened by Marie dressed in black negligée and skimpy knickers.

- Where've you been? I've been waiting for you all night, she said annoyed.
- I've been busy, he replied putting his arm around her waist and kissing her neck.

- Mmmm you know I love that, she said as her anger quickly melted away.
- Now let's get those little panties off, he said pushing her towards the bedroom.

Emma awoke the following day in a good mood. It had been a great night and Tina was very interesting. She was impressed how she was getting on with life being a young single parent. Then her mind went back to the photo entitled The Ripper Club. It was certainly strange and mysterious. Was Penny Holland really wearing Polly Nichol's bonnet? In the light of day it seemed too fantastic an idea. Who were the other three girls? Why were their faces hidden? Maybe Chris could discover more, his hacking was certainly a revelation. She got ready and headed for the college.

Later that night Tina was back on the cam-girl site. She had put Jenny to bed and dressed in her sexy lingerie was online. A typical night. She had a few regulars and a few new guys in her private chatroom. No sign of that weirdo from last night. Just after midnight Tina decided to finish and go to bed. She had made some good money so switched off her cam and logged out of her account. She was just about to turn off her computer when an email notification came through. It was unusual to receive emails this late. She started to feel uneasy. She could sense a sinister foreboding. Reaching forward she moved the mouse taking the icon towards her email inbox. She paused over it uncertain whether to open it. Her mind was racing. This was silly, how could he know her email address. Determinedly, she clicked the mouse.

JACK1888

She froze. Don't open it. Just delete it. She couldn't. An unseen force was compelling her to open it. Just delete it. The icon seemed to move of its own will over the email. Her finger hovered over the mouse button. Don't do it. Her finger came down. CLICK.

JACK1888: I saw you being a slut again tonight with little Jenny tucked up in bed. I am down on whores. I'm watching you.

Keep calm Tina. It's just some fucking sad little Troll. Don't react. That's what the little prick wants. That was the downside of being a cam-girl – attracting the attention of weirdos – but then every job has its bad side. Tina regained her composure. She put a block on JACK1888 and deleted the email. That's an end of it.

The next few days passed relatively uneventfully. The police investigation did not seem to be making any headway – another unsolved murder. Chris and Emma had come to the opinion that they had let their imaginations run wild. The chances of the Regent's Park killing having anything to do with Jack the Ripper was too fanciful. The Ripper Club picture was just girls at a fancy-dress party and the hat was just a similar one to Polly Nichol's bonnet. It had been exciting for a while though. Just leave it to the police now.

Tina was back online. She had left Jenny at her mother's flat to stay there overnight. Tina could spend the night caming and sleep late the following morning. She opened the wardrobe door and contemplated what to wear. Something provocative, she was in a dominant mood. A lot of guys liked to be dominated. She took out her black thigh length leather boots and a tight black leather skirt with a matching top. She could feel the empowerment as she rolled the boots up her legs and zipped them up. To complete the ensemble, she had a little whip with several leather strands like an old-fashioned cat o' nine tails. She thought she would have made a fine actress. It paid to be versatile as a cam girl.

Rubberman: I've been a very bad boy. I need to be punished.

Joy Boy: Do you wear PVC?

Judge Fred: Tell me I'm pathetic.

JACK1888:

Joy Boy: Do you have a strap-on?

Rubberman: I'm a gimp

Jesus Christ. There's that bastard JACK1888. No text but there he was.

Judge Fred: Humiliate me

Rubberman: I like to be tied up

JACK1888:

Joy Boy: Do you have a big black dildo?

Fuck. There he is again. Lingering in the background. Waiting. Watching. This was more than weird. It was unnerving.

Tina decided to act and put a block on JACK1888. That's the end of that.

Judge Fred: Tell me I'm a bad boy.

Jack1888: I don't like being blocked.

Tina froze. How the fuck has he got through the block? Perhaps she hadn't blocked him properly.

BLOCK JACK1888

Slowly and deliberately the texts began deleting. The curser moving backwards along each line removing each character then moving up to the next line until the page was completely blank.

What the fuck was going on thought Tina. It's this bloody computer.

A message appeared.

JACK1888: I told you I don't like being blocked.

Suddenly the lamp went out. The was cast into darkness save for the illumination from her computer screen. She trembled with fear.

JACK1888: All alone tonight? That's just the way I like it.

Tina backed away from the computer and went to the door. She turned the handle. Nothing. The door refused to move. Tina was getting frantic. She rattled the door handle up and down. She pulled it desperately. Locked. How the fuck could it be locked. Her heart was pounding with genuine fear.

JACK1888: I'm coming for you Tina.

Tina ran to the computer and turned it off. She sat there in the dark paralysed with fear. Suddenly the computer screen came back to life.

JACK1888: I'm down on whores.

Tina rushed to the door turning the handle in panic. The door opened. She just stood in shock. Was it open all the time.? She was losing her mind. The hall was pitch black. She flicked the light switch. Nothing. She stood still and listened. Nothing. Deadly silence. Get the hell out of here, she thought.

She made her way down the hall carefully in the darkness. As she approached the bathroom door the light went on inside. Tina stopped. She didn't move a muscle. Her breath quickened and her heart was racing. She had to pass the open bathroom door to get out. Tentatively she inched her way forward. Listening intensely. Nothing. She approached the open bathroom door. She stopped arid waited. Not a single sound could be heard. It was vital to get past the door and out. She steeled herself to pass the open bathroom door getting as near to the door as she could, staying close to the wall. This was it. With one decisive step she moved in front of the open doorway. Nothing. She looked inside. Nothing. She sighed with relief. Still best to go to her mum's tonight. She would go the police tomorrow.

Tina walked towards the front door in a more relaxed mood. Suddenly the bathroom light went out. She ran to the front door, scrambling for the key. Christ where is it. Then she heard approaching footsteps behind her. Please God. Her hand closed around the key. The footsteps were getting closer. She put the key in the lock and turned it. Almost there. A steely hand grabbed her hair and pulled her back as a cold steel blade plunged into her throat.

Chapter 7

There was a lot of emotion in the days following Tina's death. Lisa was too upset to work at Bar Monte Carlo. Keith had been very sympathetic and understanding. Emma mused that despite being sleazy Keith did have a caring, tender side. No-one is all bad. Despite having only met Tina on one occasion Emma had been more upset than she would have expected. She felt they had made a connection and would have become good friends. That was now lost forever.

Chris had been following the story on the news. Not many details.

The young woman found dead in her council flat in Whitechapel has been identified as Tina Stanley. She was alone in her flat when she was attacked and stabbed to death. This is the advice from the Metropolitan Police.

A solemn looking police officer in his mid-40s appeared on the screen behind a podium covered in microphones and started to speak.

We can confirm that the young woman killed on Wednesday night in Whitechapel was Tina Stanley....

A title appeared at the bottom of the screen:

METROPOLITAN POLICE SPOKESMAN DETECTIVE INSPECTOR JOHN PARNELL

Chris became alert. Detective Inspector John Parnell, the officer in charge of the Penny Holland case. This was too much to be pure co-incidence – two young women stabbed to death in the same area of London within a short space of time. He went straight to his computer to hack into Parnell's account. Having previously hacked it he knew the codes and Parnell's files appeared on the screen. He scanned down the list to the file he wanted *Stanley, Tina.* He clicked his mouse and the document opened.

Stanley, Tina

The body was discovered by Margaret Stanley, mother of the victim at 9.00am Saturday 30 October 2016. She rang police and Constables Coyle and Donald arrived at 9.15am. I was called and arrived with homicide and forensics at 9.40am.

The cadaver was severely mutilated. Forensic examination revealed that the throat had been severed deeply and that the cut was jagged and went right around the neck. The abdomen had been cut open and the intestines were severed from their attachments and lifted out and placed on the body. The uterus and bladder had been removed and could not be found at the crime scene. The incisions were cleanly cut with a very sharp knife with a thin narrow blade 8-10 inches in length. The perpetrator had good anatomical knowledge.

No signs of any break in or theft. In fact, there was £2000 in the bedside cabinet in £20 notes. Reason for money unknown. No signs of sexual activity.

The case has parallels with the Penny Holland case. Forensics believe that both killings could have been done with the same knife and by the same person.

My conclusion is that we are looking for a serial killer with medical knowledge.

Chris sat back in his chair and contemplated what he had just read. Was there a serial killer on the loose replicating the murders of Jack the Ripper? He picked up his mobile phone to ring Emma. Obviously, Emma was number 1 on his speed dial. He was just about to press 1 when he stopped. Emma had been quite upset by the murder. It would be insensitive of him to reveal the full details of the killing. The report was disturbingly graphic. He put his phone back down and thought again. He could do some research himself. That was the good side of the internet, anyone could find out anything immediately. Finding out about Jack the Ripper would be a good place to start. He sat up and searched JACK THE RIPPER. Thousands of websites. That's the other thing about the internet, separating the good sites from the bad sites. Chris wanted factual information and thought an academic website would be best, like a university. Then he had a brilliant idea. Why not find an expert? He leant over his keyboard and typed JACK THE RIPPER PATRICK BLACKBURN. Top of the search results

Patrick Blackburn: Articles on Jack the Ripper

Chris opened the website. The home page was a dim picture of a cobbled 19th century London Street. The street was narrow with hanging gas lamps on each side providing some illumination. Through the fog you could just make out the silhouette of a lone figure. He was wearing a top hat and a cape. His face was masked by the mist but in his right hand you could make out a long, narrow bladed knife.

Chris entered the site and found a menu page. The website was split into several sections: The top two sections were titled

VICTIMS and SUSPECTS. Victims would be a good place to start. Chris clicked on VICTIMS.

VICTIMS OF JACK THE RIPPER

POLLY NICHOLS

ANNIE CHAPMAN

ELIZABETH STRIDE

CATHERINE EDDOWES

MARY KELLY

Chris looked at the names. These were the five women killed by Jack the Ripper. From his conversation with Emma it had been established that the recent murder in Regent's Park of Penny Holland mirrored that of Polly Nichols. Chris was pretty sure he would find the killing of Tina Stanley mimicking that of Annie Chapman. He opened the page on Annie Chapman.

ANNIE CHAPMAN

BACKGROUND

DESCRIPTION

MURDER CHRONOLOGY

INQUEST

He clicked on INQUEST.

Testimony by Dr George Bagster

The body was terribly mutilated and the stiffness in the limbs was not marked but was evidently commencing. The throat was dissevered deeply and the incision through the skin was jagged and reached right around the neck. The instrument used at the throat and abdomen was the same. It must have been a very sharp knife with a thin narrow blade which must have been at least 6-8 inches in length, probably longer. The injuries could not have been inflicted by a bayonet. They could have been done by such an instrument as a medical man used for post-mortem purposes. There were indications of anatomical knowledge.

Chris could already see the parallels with the report of Inspector Parnell on Tina Stanley: a knife with a long narrow blade was used in both, the neck deeply severed in both. He kept reading.

The abdomen had been entirely laid open: the intestines, severed from their mesenteric attachments, had been lifted out of the body and placed on the shoulder of the corpse. From the pelvis the uterus and the bladder had been entirely removed. No trace of these parts could be found, and the incisions were cleanly cut. Obviously, the work was that of an expert or at least someone who had such knowledge of anatomical or pathological examinations as to be enabled to secure the pelvic organs with one sweep of the knife.

The more Chris read the more similarities he could see. The mutilation of the body, the removal and disappearance of organs. Both reports citing that the killer had anatomical knowledge. London was full of surgeons, doctors, nurses, medical students who would have the required skills and knowledge. His own university even had a medical faculty. He read on.

The tongue protruded between the front teeth and was much swollen. There was a bruise over the right temple. Additionally, a bruise over the middle part of the bone on the right hand. The stiffness was more noticeable on the left side, especially in the fingers which were partly closed. There was an abrasion over the ring finger with distinct markings of a ring or rings.

Chris sat back in his chair. There was a lot to think about. He wondered if Tina had any rings. He had never met her so had no idea. Emma knew her but she had been quite upset about her death. On the other hand, if there was a killer replicating the murders of Jack the Ripper and Tina was the second it was reasonable to assume there would be three more. These had to be prevented. Chris decided he had to act but with a great degree of tact. He picked up his mobile again and decided to text Emma.

CHRIS: Hi, how are you?

He would keep it casual, test the water, and take it from there. Who knew when Emma would respond anyway? Immediately was the answer.

EMMA: OK. Trying to keep busy x

So far so good.

CHRIS: How is Lisa?

EMMA: She is still upset but returning to work tomorrow x

CHRIS: How are you coping?

EMMA: It was a shock. I can't understand it x

Chris decided to push on.

CHRIS: I think I can

No reply.

Maybe that was too much too soon.

EMMA: What are you up to?

This was it.

Chris: Did Tina wear rings?

Emma: I'm on my way over.

An hour later Chris and Emma were sat in the living room.

- So, what have you discovered? asked Emma.
- I've been doing some research on Jack the Ripper.
- What have you found out?
- That the murder of Annie Chapman by Jack the Ripper resembles Tina's.
- Have you been hacking the police report again? That inspector Parnell.
- Yes. Do you want to see it?
- No, said Emma quickly with a degree of emotion.

Chris could see by her face that reading the details would be too disturbing for Emma. Reading about the murder of a stranger was very different to reading about the killing of someone you knew. With the death of a stranger you could be detached and objective but closer to home was certainly a more emotional experience.

- You asked about rings, enquired Emma composing herself.

- Did Tina wear any rings?
- Yes. Three brass rings. I noticed them and made a remark about them the night I met Tina. She said they were her grandmother's.
- The police also discovered £2,000 in her bedside cabinet. I wonder what she was doing with that and where she got it from.

Emma was silent and pensive. She was not keen to say Tina was a cam girl. Even so it was unlikely that she was paid in cash.

- Perhaps she withdrew it from her bank account for something, ventured Emma.
- Possibly. I could try to find out, but I would need to know her bank and account number.
- Are you thinking of hacking her account? asked Emma apprehensively.
- It's a lead we can follow. Additionally, since I hacked the police we are already down the rabbit hole.
- Ok. How are we going to get her bank details?
- Well the easiest way is to see a statement or get her bank card.
- Her mother would have her possessions, I guess.
- Ok. We need to go and see her mother, said Chris.
- We can't just turn up at her doorstep and ask to see her dead daughter's bank details. Furthermore, I've never met her mother.
- I bet Lisa has.

Emma knew that was true. Lisa and Tina had been friends since childhood. Then again, she was not keen to involve Lisa in this.

- Lisa doesn't need to know what's going on, said Chris who wanted to involve as few people as possible.
- I know she has been to her mother's regularly since the incident.
- Ok. That's our path in.

Emma took out her mobile and rang Lisa. While the girls chatted Chris was thinking. He had to get Tina's bank details. He would also like to see these brass rings.

- Hi Lisa. How are you?
- I'm getting better not so much crying.
- What are you doing today?
- I'm going to see Mrs Stanley.

Emma knew this was fortuitous timing.

- I could go with you if you want? she offered.
- That would be nice. You're such a good friend Em.

Emma felt a sudden pang of guilt about using Lisa to get to Tina's mother. She was not a devious person and did not like deceiving Lisa but she would be acting altruistically. Finding Tina's killer was the highest of motives she reasoned to herself and if Chris was right it would prevent the killing of more girls. Emma steeled herself, this killer had to be stopped by any means.

- Ok. I am going to accompany Lisa to Tina's mother's house.
- When? asked Chris.
- Now.
- Good. I'll get my coat.
- You want to come too? said Emma surprised.
- Of course.

- That's going to be two strangers turning up at the door.
- Look., we need one person to search for the bank details and one to keep the others occupied.
- Why don't you just hack her bank details like you do everything else anyway?
- Banks are the hardest systems to hack. You can hack government agencies and discover national secrets, but money is guarded tightly.
- Fine. Let's go then.

Soon Chris, Emma and Lisa were sat in the living room of Tina's mother's home. It was a council flat in a tower block not far from Tina's. Being a small flat would make it easier to search than a house thought Chris.

- I'm so sorry Mrs Stanley, said Emma sympathetically.
- Thank you dear, replied Mrs Stanley.
- How is Jenny?
- She still doesn't know anything about it. I don't know what I'm going to say to her, she said distraught at the thought.

Chris was scanning the living room as they chatted. Quite a small room. A small worn sofa that Emma and Lisa were sitting on facing a huge plasma television. There was a small dining table with two metal chairs, one at each end where Chris and Mrs Stanley were now sitting. On the wall beside him hung several framed photos. A young girl in a summer dress, undoubtedly Jenny. Another of Jenny in a school uniform. Another of Jenny as a baby in a young women's arms. This must have been Tina as a teenager. Chris leant towards the picture for a closer look. As he scanned the photo something drew his attention. On the middle finger of her left hand were three brass rings.

- That was taken just after Jenny was born, said Mrs Stanley who could see Chris examining the photo. - She was a beautiful baby.
- Yes, I can see, said Chris who could not really see that at all. As far as he could see all babies looked the same. Besides he was interested in something else. – Unusual rings she's wearing.

Emma held her breath. Chris was certainly not wasting time.

- Her grandmother gave them to her, said Mrs Stanley.
- They belonged to her grandmother? pressed Chris.
- Yes, and her grandmother before that. Personally, I think they are ugly.
- Do you still have them? ventured Chris trying to mask his eagerness.
- No. I don't know where they are now. - All her personal effects are here in her old bedroom.
- I took that photo, said Lisa with tears welling up in her eyes.

Emma put her arm around Lisa to comfort her. Chris sat back silently in his chair, his mind racing. The rings were clearly missing. Undoubtedly taken by the killer as a macabre souvenir. Could they be more than just souvenirs? Are they in fact the same rings that belonged to Annie Chapman? Additionally, if Tina's personal effects were here that would probably include her bank card. He had to search and do it now. He took out his mobile phone below the table and secretly typed a text to Emma.

I'm going to search through Tina's things. Keep them in this room

Emma read the message and looked at Chris. She gave a subtle nod.

- Can I use the bathroom? asked Chris.
- Certainly, replied Mrs Stanley. – It's the first door on the right.

Chris went into the narrow hallway ensuring he closed the sitting room door behind him. His eyes scanned the corridor quickly. There were six doors off the hallway including the sitting room door. First right was the bathroom he had already been told. Judging by the fixed position handles of the two doors each end left were cupboards. He knew the kitchen was off the living room which meant middle left and far right were bedrooms: Mrs Stanley's and Tina's. Far right seemed to be the smallest so that was probably Tina's. He had to act fast. He moved quickly to the door and opened it. Chris could see by the posters of pop stars on the wall that this was Tina's room as a teenager. He closed the door behind him. On the floor was a small cardboard box with Tina's personal possessions. He crouched down and rummaged through them. A handbag. He emptied the contents. Assorted make up and keys. No doubt keys to Tina's flat. Probably spares if they have been left in a box reasoned Chris. They might come in useful. Chris put them in his pocket. He kept searching. Bingo. A purse. He opened it. Credit cards, gym membership card, bank card. He took his phone out and took a photo of the card. No need to take the card, he only wanted the account details. He put everything back in the box. Something on the bedside table caught his eye. It was a small jewellery box. He picked it up and opened it. Necklaces, bracelets, he emptied it onto the bed. No brass rings. Where were they?

BLIP

A text message. He looked at his phone.

Emma: *MRS STANLEY!*

He heard the living room door open then footsteps coming down the hall. Where was she going? Footsteps getting nearer. Chris held his breath. He could hide under the bed but what use would that do with the jewellery spread out on the bed. The footsteps stopped outside the door. Chris stood motionless. He heard the door open of the cupboard opposite. He dared not breath. The door closed and the footsteps retreated back down the hall. Chris let out a huge sigh of relief as he heard the living room door open. He listened intently. He could hear their voices. The door was still open. He would be seen if he left the bedroom. He texted Emma.

Chris: *Close the door*

He waited and listened.

- They are nice photos, said Emma getting up and approaching the wall where they hung.
- They are my favourites, replied Mrs Stanley
- I like this one of Jenny, continued Emma casually pushing the door shut.

Chris packed the jewellery into the box as fast as he could and put it back in its original place. He moved swiftly from the bedroom closing the door and into the bathroom, determined that every detail of the subterfuge should be effective to avoid arousing any suspicions. Additionally, he did not want to be thought of as unhygienic. He flushed the toilet, ran the hot water tap for a few seconds and opened the living room door.

- She's a beautiful girl, remarked Emma who was stood by the door still admiring the photos.

Clever, thought Chris.

- We'd better go, said Chris.
- I'll stay for a bit, said Lisa.

Emma gave her a hug and left with Chris.

- Did you get it? asked Emma once outside.
- The bank details, yes, but there is no sign of the rings.

Back at Chris's flat they sat in the living room.

- So, where does this leave us? asked Emma.
- Well, we know the killing of Tina is a copy-cat killing of Jack the Ripper and his second victim Annie Chapman.
- And we know Tina had three brass rings the same as Annie Chapman and that they are missing. Do you think they are Annie Chapman's rings?
- Almost certainly, said Chris pensively. – We know they were given to Tina by her grand-mother. We can assume the killer also knows that.
- I can do some more research on Annie Chapman, offered Emma.
- Ok. While you're doing that I can try to hack into Tina's bank account. I just get the feeling that £2.000 is important.
- I need to go now, said Emma looking at her watch. – I'm covering Lisa's shift in the bar tonight.

- Ok. Let me know when you discover something.

Emma got up and kissed Chris on the cheek before leaving. As Chris was left alone he was conscious that that was the first time Emma had kissed him

Chapter 8

A usual night in Bar Monte Carlo, Keith and his cronies standing at the bar leering at girls half their age. The usual sexual innuendo and groping for any girl who strayed too close to the pack. Although Keith did get a few of the bimbos into bed. That's the power of owning a trendy bar mused Emma, power as an aphrodisiac. As Emma observed them they were suddenly almost drooling with their eyes on stalks. Emma turned to see what bimbo was the cause of all this excitement. Across the bar she saw Jane Ericsson. Emma understood immediately. Jane was wearing thigh length black leather boots with a 6-inch stiletto heel. A short black lycra skirt stretched tightly across her buttocks and a red blouse with the obligatory top buttons undone to display her cleavage and a seductive red neckerchief. Emma wondered if she had applied her make up with a trowel. Her lips were covered with thick scarlet lipstick and looking at her eye shadow and mascara Emma pondered if she had just done three rounds with Mohammed Ali.

- Jane you look as hot as ever, said Keith putting his arm around her and pulling her close so he could feel her firm breasts against his body.
- Hot enough for you to by me a drink, teased Jane seductively. She knew how to play men like Keith.
- Of course, whatever you desire, smarmed Keith putting his hand on her arse.
- I think a cocktail, she said putting the emphasis on the word cock.

- I'll give you a cocktail, said Keith also emphasising cock.
- I feel like *Sex-on-the-beach.*

Emma thought Keith was going to have a heart attack he was getting so excited. He motioned to the barman.

- I'll be sitting over there, said Jane nodding at an empty booth and removing herself from Keith's eager hands.
- I'll bring it over personally, said Keith admiring her arse as she walked away.

Nearing the end of the night the bar was thinning out. Jane was quite drunk having been plied with drink by Keith with the aim of getting her into bed. They were sat in the booth, Keith with is arm around her and Jane loving the attention and the free drink. Although how much of Keith's drivel she was listening to Emma was unsure. Every time she had glanced over Jane was staring at her mobile phone. This was something that drove Emma crazy – people who constantly look at their mobile phones, especially when they are out with others. She had earlier observed a group of girls her age in the bar all staring at their phones. No conversation. They might as well have just stayed at home thought Emma. Do we all live in our own bubble? She read somewhere that people look at their mobile phones an average of over 120 times a day. What were they looking at? Chris would be certain they were looking at "bloody pictures of coffee cups and cakes". That thought made Emma smile to herself. That's what she liked about Chris, he didn't get his mobile phone out and stare at it when she was with him. She could actually have an uninterrupted conversation with him. Chris said it was because he didn't have any friends. Emma gave a little laugh. She was sure that was a joke. Well, almost sure.

- Emma, when you're finished entertaining yourself can you ask Keith to check tonight's takings, said one of the barmen who had clearly been watching her.
- Certainly, she said going a little red.

She approached the booth.

- Excuse me, Keith. Can you check tonight's takings?

Keith looked a little peeved at having to stop his groping of Jane.

- I'll be right back, said Keith standing up. – Don't go anywhere honey.
- I'll be waiting, replied Jane batting her eyelashes.

Keith blew her a kiss and ambled off to the bar.

- Join me, she beckoned Emma tapping the couch beside her.
- I can't right now. I'm working, replied Emma not keen to be subjected to Jane's drunken rambling.
- Aww come on, she said leaning over, grabbing Emma's arm and pulling her into the booth. – Keith won't mind. He'd do anything for me.

No doubt thought Emma.

- He fancies me, she said taking a huge slurp from her glass. – He fancies all the girls. He's a real player.

Emma didn't need anyone to tell her that.

- Do you know he's on dating sites? I mean sex dating sites. You know…for casual sex.
- How do you know? asked Emma.
- I've seen his profile.

- Where?
- On sex dating sites.
- How?
- Well, I'm on there too. Everyone is on them.

Emma knew that was not true. For a start off she was not on them. She seriously doubted that Chris was on them.

- Do you want to see his profile?
- Not really, replied Emma keen to move away but Jane leaning drunkenly against her.
- Hold on, said Jane fumbling around with her phone.
- I need to go Jane, urged Emma trying to extricate herself.
- Here it is.

Emma looked down. Sure enough, there he was, his big grinning stupid face in some kind of James Bond pose that he probably thought was the height of cool but just made him look like a knob.

- It's great for sex, said Jane. – I meet loads of guys. You should try it.
- No thanks.
- But don't use your real name
- What name do you use?
- Valkyrie. You know from Norse myshology, said Jane slurring her words
- What?
- Myshology
- Mythology, corrected Emma.
- Myshology. Tha's what I said.
- Yes, I know, they took the dead warriors from the battlefield to Valhalla.

- More than just that, they decide who lives and who dies. Also, they fuck heroes.
- Yes, I know. They were the lovers of heroes, said Emma phrasing it more poetically.
- Not that there are many heroes on the sex site. You get a lot of explishit pics.
- What?
- Explishit.
- Explicit? ventured Emma wearily.
- Yea. Tha's what I said. Look, here's Keith's cock.

Emma looked quickly away. She had no desire to see Keith's cock.

- Don't you think it looks like a small banana? Except, it's not yellow.

Jane went into a paroxysm of laughter at that. Emma pushed her away and stood up.

- Got to go, Jane. See you tomorrow, she said as she hurried away leaving Jane sprawled out on the booth couch giggling like an idiot.

Chris had been trying all night to hack into Tina's bank account but to no avail. You could hack into police records and national defence but banks were nigh on impossible. It just confirmed what Chris always suspected – money was valued more highly than lives. He would keep trying of course, Chris was persistent and liked a challenge, there was always a way. Perhaps Emma would have better luck with her research.

When Emma got back from work it was late but she was not particularly tired. She switched on her computer and searched: ANNIE CHAPMAN

Thousands of results. Emma narrowed the search: ANNIE CHAPMAN BACKGROUND.

She clicked on a website and started reading.

Born Annie Elizabeth Smith 1 September 1841

Father George Smith. Mother Ruth Chapman

Annie married John Chapman, a coachman on 1 May 1869. Residence on marriage certificate 29 Montpelier Place, Brompton, London.

They had three children named Emily, Annie and John.

The couple separated in 1884 or 1885. Exact date unknown.

In 1886 she lived with John Sivvey at 30 Dorset Street, Spitalfields, London.

Sometime in 1887 to 1888 she started a relationship with a bricklayer's mate who lived at 1 Osborn Place. Unconfirmed rumours that Annie had a child with this man.

Emma's eyes widened as she read the name of this man.

EDWARD STANLEY

Emma was stunned. Could it be that Tina Stanley was the direct descendent of Annie Chapman? Despite the late hour she got her phone out and texted Chris.

Emma: *Big news. See you tomorrow XX*

Chapter 9

Early the following morning they were all in Professor Bury's room for another tutorial. Jane looked hung over with huge black bags under her eyes due to the excessive drinking in Bar Monte Carlo the previous evening. She was dressed down in jeans and a fleece. Clearly in no mood for flirting today. Will jumped on this with sadistic glee.

- No skirt today Jane? Did you leave it in Bar Monte Carlo last night, possibly hanging off one of the lamp shades?
- Fuck off, murmured Jane slumped in her chair.
- Did you spend the night riding Hammy the Hamster?
- Leave her alone Will, sad Emma jumping to her defence. She did not always like the things Jane did or said but she could not abide Will.
- What's the matter Emma? Are you jealous? I'm sure Keith could have accommodated you in a threesome.
- You really are an arsehole, said Jane attempting to pull herself upright in her chair but failing and slumping back down.

Emma wanted to punch him in the face. Liam just sat there silently watching and listening. There's never a hero around when you need one thought Emma.

Professor Bury entered the room and the group fell silent.

- Before we start today, he announced – Patrick has asked me to give you this.

He handed the students a flyer. Emma looked it and read:

ULTIMATE QUEST

Students with agile and curious minds are invited to participate in solving the greatest mystery of all time. A puzzle that has challenged the most astute minds for over 100 years.

Who was Jack the Ripper?

Meet at Patrick Blackburn's room, 6pm today

This was a new development thought Emma. Should she go? Would it help her and Chris's secret investigation into the recent murders?

- I wouldn't get too hopeful of solving the mystery of who Jack the Ripper was, said Professor Bury. – However, there could be some interesting psychological observations from Patrick.
- I don't think we can learn anything new about Jack the Ripper, dismissed Liam.
- I don't know, countered Will. – It's an interesting story.
- Since when are you interested in Jack the Ripper? Challenged Jane trying to sit up straight in her chair and failing again.
- I studied the case as a teenager, said Will. – I think I'll go along.

Emma sat in stunned silence. This was unlike Will to show any interest in anything outside of class that was not wearing a skirt. And it was unlike Liam, who normally just sat quietly, to express a forceful opinion, just writing it off as a waste of time. Had the universe tipped upside down?

- I'll go too, mumbled Jane hoping to see Will make a total arse of himself. – After I've had a little nap.

Emma met Chris in the refectory for lunch.

- How did you get on with the bank account? asked Emma in a hushed voice so as not to be over-heard.
- That's a no go at the moment, he replied looking down disappointedly. - I can't hack the codes but I'm still working on it.
- Never mind, said Emma re-assuringly putting her hand on his arm.

Chris looked at Emma's hand on his arm. He was not by nature a tactile person so was always aware of any body contact. He could feel the warmth radiating through Emma's palm and he liked it.

- I have made some interesting discoveries, she continued.
- Tell me, said Chris focusing his mind.
- I did some research on Annie Chapman. About a year before her death she had a relationship. The name of the man was Edward Stanley.

Chris raised his eyebrows.

- There's more. There were unconfirmed rumours that the couple had a child.
- Good work. I think we have made a connection between Tina Stanley and Annie Chapman. If we can now find a link between Penny Holland and Polly Nichols, we will have established a pattern.
- I've got something else, said Emma pausing
- What? replied Chris sitting forward on his seat in anticipation.
- Patrick Blackburn is forming a group to investigate Jack the Ripper.
- What is the purpose of the group?
- To solve the mystery. To identify Jack the Ripper.

Chris sat back deep in thought.

- Do you think it would help us if I went? asked Emma.
- Yes. I think these recent killings are somehow tied up with the Ripper story.
- The first meeting is this evening.
- Go. Learn what you can. In the meantime, I'll do some research on Penny Holland.
- Ok. We'll meet up later.

Emma leant forward and kissed him on the cheek before leaving.

That's two noted Chris.

It was already getting dark when Emma got to Patrick's room. She was a bit late but need not have hurried. It was a meagre turn out, three people. Perhaps Liam had been right and it was a futile exercise chasing shadows from 1888. He was certainly conspicuous by his absence. Patrick was dressed all in black as usual. Will was looking as smug as ever and Jane was looking more alive than this morning. She had put on extra make up to mask the bags under her eyes and was back in a short skirt. They were sat around the desk with papers spread out over it. Emma sat down. Patrick started.

- Jack the Ripper killed five women in Whitechapel in the autumn of 1888.
- Five prostitutes, corrected Will in his usual arrogant manner.
- Polly Nichols 31 August, Annie Chapman 8 September, Elizabeth Stride and Catherine Eddowes, both 30 September, and Mary Kelly 9 November, continued Patrick ignoring Will. - What everyone wants to know is who was he?
- Severin Klosowski, interrupted Will.
- Really? said Patrick with a supercilious smirk on his face.
- Also known as George Chapman – no relation to Annie Chapman
- Yes. I know him.
- He was in Whitechapel in 1888.
- So were all the other suspects, dismissed Patrick.
- Yes, but he had only just arrived in London from Poland. Furthermore, he had trained as a surgeon whilst in Poland.
- Quite so.
- The way the bodies were mutilated with internal organs removed it has to be agreed that the killer had surgical knowledge.

- Yes, the killer had to have good surgical knowledge but Klosowski was hanged for poisoning three of his wives on 7 April 1903.
- Further evidence that he was a killer of women.
- Yes, but the wives were poisoned whereas Jack the Ripper stabbed his victims to death. Serial killers do not change their method of killing. Also, they don't suddenly stop killing so what was he doing between the last killing of Mary Kelly in November 1888 and his arrest in October 1902, taking a holiday?

Jane grinned. She was enjoying watching Will being dismissed and wriggling like a worm on a hook. She should have brought popcorn.

- Klosowski was the favoured suspect of the officer in charge of the investigation, Inspector Abberline, added Will trying to salvage his argument and conscious he was losing.
- Montague John Druitt was the favoured suspect of Chief Constable Sir Melville Macnaghten. Assistant Commissioner Sir Robert Anderson believed it was Kosminski.

The room fell silent. Will seemed to have gone into a sulk. Jane was hoping and praying he would say something else that Patrick could rubbish.

- I've heard of Druitt, ventured Emma breaking the silence.
- Go on, invited Patrick whose eyes seemed to be gleaming ready to devour another student.
- As you say he was linked to the killings. His decomposed body was pulled from the Thames on 31

December 1888. It was believed his body had been in the river for several weeks which would place his death at the beginning of December.

- His tombstone records the death as 4 December 1888.
- If he was Jack the Ripper this would account for the end of the killings.
- Quite so, conceded Patrick.
- Chief Constable Sir Melville Macnaghten stated Druitt was Jack the Ripper.
- What he actually claimed was that that Druitt's family thought he was the killer.
- Scotland Yard's records say he was a doctor which would account for his expertise dissecting his victims.
- Scotland's Yards records are wrong. He was a barrister and part time teacher. However, his father was a doctor so he could have acquired some knowledge from him. Druitt was very intelligent. He had been educated at Winchester and New College, Oxford.
- I don't think that would enable him to remove organs as Jack the Ripper did, chipped in Jane.
- You think not? replied Patrick. – Will, I believe your father is a Harley Street surgeon.
- Yes, said Will surprised. – How do you know that?
- Have you seen him operate?
- Yes. I've been to the hospital many times.
- I suspect Druitt had seen his father operate too.
- Ok, he had medical knowledge, conceded Jane - but he was insane.
- Insanity did run in the Druitt family, said Patrick. - His mother was a patient in the Manor House Asylum.
- I would say being insane makes him a more likely suspect to be Jack the Ripper, concluded Emma.

- I've always thought Kosminski was a more likely suspect, said Jane.
- Enlighten us, invited Will seeing his chance to get back at her.
- Well he was insane also. He had been in Colney Hatch Lunatic Asylum. He lived in Whitechapel in 1888 and was a Jew.
- So what? said Will.
- Additionally, in 2014 DNA analysis attempted to link Kosminski to a shawl belonging to Catherine Eddowes.
- The results were inconclusive, dismissed Will.
- There was the writing on the wall, *The Jews are the men that will not be blamed for nothing*.
- I've heard of that, said Emma.
- It was discovered by police written in white chalk on a wall in Goulston Street, Whitechapel 30 September 1888 after the murders of Stride and Eddowes, explained Jane. – Below it was a torn blood-stained piece of cloth that was identified as being part of the shawl worn by Eddowes.
- What does this mean? asked Emma.
- That the killer was a Jew like Kosminski.
- Not necessarily, countered Patrick – More important is why did the police scrub the message?

The room fell silent. This was all very interesting but how was this helping Emma in her real quest. They all certainly knew a lot about Jack the Ripper but what did that prove?

- Klosowski, Druitt and Kosminski all have links to Whitechapel 1888 but there is one suspect who was hardly mentioned at the time, said Patrick. - Francis Tumblety

The group remained silent. Patrick continued.

- Tumblety was an American who lived in Whitechapel in 1888. He was known to be trying to buy uteri in London and, in fact, did himself have medical knowledge. In 1857 he was arrested for attempting an abortion on a prostitute but the charges were dropped. However, it was evidence of his medical knowledge. He was arrested again in London 7 November 1888 for gross indecency and indecent assault. While on bail he fled to France 24 November 1888, 17 days after the murder of the last Ripper victim, Mary Kelly. I find it strange that he was never mentioned by name in connection with the Whitechapel killings.
- No-one will ever know, said Jane.
- I don't agree, said Patrick. – I think people knew at the time.
- What do you mean? asked Emma.
- It was a cover up, claimed Patrick. – I have researched Jack the Ripper for years. Macnaghten claimed in 1913 that he knew the identity of Jack the Ripper but destroyed the documents. I believe these documents still exist.

Chris sat at his computer and researched Polly Nichols. He had to find a connection between Nichols and Penny Holland. Nichols was born Mary Ann Walker. Strange co-incidence, he thought, Walker, same as myself. He continued reading.

Brown eyes, dark complexion, brown hair, small scar on forehead from childhood injury. "A very clean woman who always seemed to keep to herself", said Emily Holland.

That was it. The link between Nichols and Penny Holland. Chris appraised what he had discovered so far. The names of the victims were all connected. The murders of Penny and Tina were not random acts. The killer was targeting them specifically. Who? Let's see who Penny Holland had contact with. Chris hacked into her email account. He scrolled down the emails. Suddenly he stopped at a name he recognised.

Keith Hammond

He opened it.

Keith: *Book me in for tonight at 10*

That didn't surprise Chris. Penny had been a prostitute and Keith struck Chris as the kind of guy who would use prostitutes. Chris made a note of the connection. However, having met Keith he did not strike Chris as having the required intelligence to trace the past to the present. This was complex. Whoever it was had made the connection between the present and the past. This person would be clever and calculating. Chris scrolled down the emails once more. And there it was – Will Dumas. An email from a few months ago. Chris opened the email.

Will: *You cheap whore. No-one dumps me by email. I'll kill you.*

There must be a sent email, thought Chris. He noted the date and opened the sent email box. Same date but earlier email to Will Dumas.

Penny: *We're over Will. I don't like being two-timed. I know you were with Tina.*

So, Will had been in a relationship with Penny Holland and also had a liaison with Tina. He pulled up Tina's Facebook. He scrolled down. No pictures of Will. Perhaps it was only a one-night stand. Then something stopped his train of thought. A picture, a picture he had seen before, The Ripper Club.

Chapter 10

Jane was back at her flat bored. Her parents were rich which meant she could afford to rent a flat by herself and not share with anyone. She was still feeling the effects of the drink from the previous night so was not in the mood to study. The meeting in Patrick's room had been fun, she loved watching Will suffer. He was so full of himself, it was good to see him taken down a peg or two. Although, he had been a good fuck. This memory made her suddenly feel horny. A bit of flirting online would be good. She lay on her bed and picked up her mobile. There was bound to be a hot guy on the sex dating site. Valkyrie logging on, said Jane to herself. Now just sit back and wait. Within minutes she was inundated with likes and invitations.

Hung Hank: Hi gorgeous. Where do you live?

Delete. Too fast. She didn't want any weirdos just turning up at her flat.

Horny Toad: I want to fuck you tonight.

Delete. His face looks a bit like a toad and I don't need someone sliming all over me thank you very much.

Sharky Shark: Hi xx

Delete. He looks ok, but that name is a bit childish. Probably has a small penis.

Saucy J: Hi Valkyrie. I would like you to escort me to Valhalla xx

This looks more promising thought Jane, clearly intelligent as he knows what a Valkyrie is. Interesting photo. Maintaining an air of mystery with a black mask over his eyes and red bandana. Could be a weirdo though thought Jane. She wasn't keen on the name Saucy J either. Yet she was intrigued.

Valkyrie: Hi xx

Saucy J: Hi xx. Are you as exotic as your name?

Valkyrie: Exotic and erotic xx

Saucy J: Yes, I can see by your picture, a true Valkyrie, lover to heroes xx

Valkyrie: I'm always looking for a hero xx

Saucy J: I could be your hero and you could be my Valkyrie xx

Valkyrie: Mmm xx

Saucy J: Gently kiss your soft red lips

Valkyrie: Mmmmmm

Saucy J: Slowly strip you and run my strong hands over your naked body

Valkyrie: Oh yes xx

Saucy J: Moving my hands over your nubile body as I kiss your cherry lips

Jane was getting turned on.

Saucy J: Cup your firm breasts in my warm hands, gently teasing your nipples with my fingertips.

Valkyrie: Oh yea xx

Saucy j: You like that Valkyrie

Valkyrie: I do xx

Saucy J: I'd like to meet you and do that for real xx

Valkyrie: We'll see. Tell me what else you will do to me xx

Saucy J: I think that's enough for now xx

Jane felt frustrated but seduced at the same time.

Saucy J: I'll text you again soon.

Valkyrie: Yes, please do

Saucy J: Bye for now xx

Valkyrie: Before you go, what's your name?

Saucy J: Call me Jack.

Chris was busy running his code breaking programme trying to access Tina's bank account again. There had to be a way, there was always a way. He looked up as Emma entered his room.

- I didn't hear you knock.
- Liam let me in. He was going out just as a I arrived.
- How was the meeting?
- Interesting, replied Emma. – They certainly all knew a lot about Jack the Ripper. Patrick I expected but Will and Jane knew a surprising amount.
- Go on.

- Well, they discussed the usual suspects: Druitt, Klosowski and Kosminski.
- Did you make any progress in solving the mystery?
- Not really, although Patrick said something interesting.
- What?
- He said that Scotland Yard knew who Jack the Ripper was but had covered it up.
- Why would they do that? asked Chris intrigued.
- He didn't say but he claimed that secret documents existed proving it.
- Interesting. Did you discover anything to help us in the present?
- Not exactly. Patrick claimed Jack the Ripper had medical knowledge but this did not mean he had to be a doctor of surgeon. He suggested an astute person could have learnt the required skills by merely being present and observing operations.
- Maybe, agreed Chris.
- He then went on to imply that Will could do it as he had observed his surgeon father operate.

Chris furrowed his brow deep in thought.

- Have you discovered anything? asked Emma breaking his concentration.
- Yes, quite a bit. I've found a link between Penny Holland and Polly Nichols. There was a friend of Polly Nichols named Emily Holland.
- Good so we have Tina connected to Annie Chapman and now Penny connected to Polly Nichols.
- There's more. I found an email from Keith Hammond to Penny. It seems he was meeting her for sexual services.

- I know he's sleazy but a killer?
- He's not the only familiar name I found.

Emma moved to the edge of her seat in eager anticipation.

- Will Dumas, said Chris. – Did you know he had been out with Penny and also had some sort of liaison with Tina?
- No, said Emma astonished.
- It seems he had a fling with Tina while seeing Penny.
- I'm not surprised about that. I've seen the way he acts in Bar Monte Carlo chatting up women. - It's Lisa I feel sorry for.
- I found an email from Will to Penny threatening to kill her after she dumped him.
- He's a misogynist prick, said Emma getting angry thinking about him and remembering how he had threatened her in the cellar. He was clearly one of those men who do not like being rejected and get aggressive when they are.
- I found another connection between Penny and Tina.
- What is it?
- I'll show you.

Chris opened the Facebook page of Tina Stanley and scrolled down to the photo.

- It's the same photo as Penny had, gasped Emma wide eyed.
- Exactly.
- And that title again, "The Ripper Club". What does it mean?
- I think it's significant, asserted Chris.
- Who are the girls?

- That's what we need to find out.
- Well we know the girl left of centre is Penny Holland. The other three could be anybody.
- I don't think so, said Chris mysteriously. – Look closer at the girl on the right.

Emma looked closely. She was wearing a brown bodice laced up the middle and a black skirt down to her ankles. The clothes were antiquated, typical Victorian dress of the end of the 19th century. Sturdy looking black shoes barely visible under the skirt. Her face was obscured by her purple fan that she held in front of her face.

- Can you zoom in on the fan? she asked Chris.

Chris outlined the fan and zoomed in, enlarging that segment of the photo. There were three small holes at the bottom of the fan.

- Zoom in on the holes?

Chris zoomed in and enlarged the holes. The photo became blurry.

- Can you make it clearer?
- Maybe a bit.

Chris framed the section and brightened it. Emma moved her head closer to the screen.

- It's hard to see, said Emma straining her eyes. - It's something reddish.
- Her hair? ventured Chris.
- Maybe. Go back to the original size.

Emma looked again at the girl. She had started to guess who it was.

- Can you focus on the hand on her hip?

Chris focused on the hand.

- Enlarge.

Emma could clearly see the girl's fingers from the tips to the middle joints but the rear portion was unclear. There was something there though.

- Rotate photo

The photo rotated. Emma looked closely. Three brass rings. Tina.

Emma contemplated what they had discovered - a photo with two girls with items belonging to victims of Jack the Ripper who were now dead themselves. Who were the other two girls in the picture? The next to be killed? A sudden buzzing broke Emma's thoughts.

- It's the bank account. We're in, said Chris excitedly. – Let's see if we can find out where she got the £2000 that was in her flat the night she died.

They gathered around the computer screen. Chris brought up Tina's most recent bank statement. The usual cash withdrawals but nothing for £2000. The usual expenses: council tax, gas and electricity, mobile phone, internet. Nothing of interest there. He looked at the final transaction.

CREDIT: TWILIGHT ENTERTAINMENT £1760

- That's strange, said – Chris. - I wonder what that is.

Emma remained silent.

Chris brought up the previous month's statement.

CREDIT: TWILIGHT ENTERTAINMENT £1840

He went back two months.

CREDIT: TWILIGHT ENTERTAINMENT £1780

- Whatever it is it's a regular payment. Look, it's a different amount but always paid on the same day each month. It must be a job of some kind. I thought she didn't work because she had a small child?
- She did have a sort of job, admitted Emma tentatively.
- What? asked Chris astonished at this sudden revelation.
- She worked from home.
- Doing what?
- A cam girl.
- A cam girl?
- Yes.
- Why didn't you say before?
- I didn't like to spread it around after her murder.
- It could be important Emma. Do you know the name of the website she used?
- No, mumbled Emma guiltily that she had not told Chris before.
- Ok, said Chris smiling. Emma was very caring, she had a good heart. – We still don't know where the £2000 came from. I want to go to Tina's flat.
- What for?
- I want to see what's on her computer. Specifically, the cam girl site.

- Can't you hack it from here?
- No. Firstly, we don't know which site it is and secondly, we wouldn't be able to see any chat history.
- So, you're just going to break into her flat, said Emma incredulously. This was taking them onto new and more perilous ground.
- Not exactly, I have a set of keys. I took them from her mother's flat when we were there, I thought they might come in useful.
- When do you want to go there?
- Tonight.

Emma was apprehensive.

- It needs to be tonight. If everything we believe is true, the killer will strike again and soon.
- Ok. Tonight.

****

It was pitch black when they arrived at Tina's flat. Chris was carrying a small shoulder bag.

- What's in the bag? asked Emma
- Everything we will need.

Chris opened the door with the stolen keys and fished a small torch out of the bag.

- You've thought of everything, whispered Emma observing the torch. – If things don't work out in computing you can always take up burglary.

They made their way down the hall, Chris scanning with the torch. He opened the first door and shone the light inside. The bathroom. He closed the door and moved on down the hall. He opened the second door. Bedroom. He shone the light around the room. There was a double bed in the centre of the room with a desk in front on it. He focused on the desk. Bingo. The closed laptop was sitting on top. They approached the desk. Chris sat down and opened the laptop and turned it on while Emma stood behind him. The screen flickered to life. He opened the website history. Last website opened X-CAM LIVE.

- This must be it, said Chris.

He opened it and a login page appeared. Chris took his code breaking device from his bag and connected it to the laptop.

- This should be easy as we are using Tina's computer.

Within seconds they were in.

- She seems to have gone by the name Roxanne, observed Chris.

He opened the chat history. The screen was blank.

- There's nothing there, said Emma puzzled.
- That's strange, the last conversation should be here.
- Perhaps the website people removed them.
- It would be easier just to delete the account.
- What do you think? said Emma putting her hand on his shoulder.
- I think this laptop has been hacked, concluded Chris sombrely. – I'm going to see what's on the hard drive.

He opened the hard drive history. They both looked at the entries.

JACK1888: I told you I don't like being blocked.

JACK1888: All alone tonight? That's just the way I like it.

JACK1888: I'm coming for you Tina.

JACK1888: I'm down on whores.

As Emma read the texts the room suddenly felt like a cold and empty place. A chill went down her spine. It hit her that this was the scene of a cruel, calculated slaying. These were the words of a merciless killer. She could picture the sheer terror that had occurred here.

- Let's go, she implored Chris.
- Ok. I don't think we can learn anymore here.

He unplugged his code breaker and turned the laptop off. He picked up the torch. Suddenly his eye caught something laying on the bedside table. He shone the torch onto it. Tina's mobile phone. He walked over to it.

- Chris. Let's go, urged Emma

Chris quickly picked the phone up, put it in his bag and followed Emma out through the door. They walked back to Emma's room in the hall of residence to consider what they had discovered this evening.

- The killer obviously used the name JACK1888, stated Chris.
- It's clearly a reference to Jack the Ripper and the year he killed the five women, said Emma.

- Those messages were sent the night Tina was killed. In fact, I would say they were sent immediately prior to her murder. I think the killer was already in the flat.
- How is that possible?
- It could be done from any device that was connected to the internet and Tina's laptop. Most probably something small and portable like a tablet or a high technology mobile phone. Whoever the killer is he has good computer skills and knows how to hack.

Emma was silent, contemplating what they had so far. A killer with good computer hacking skills, medical knowledge and knowledge of Jack the Ripper. She looked at Chris who had a mobile phone in his hand.

- What's that?
- Tina's phone. I saw it in the bedroom.

He observed the concerned look on Emma's face.

- We are in too deep to turn back now, he said.

He opened the text history. Day of murder.

Mum: No need to cook dinner for Jenny this evening I bought fish. See you at 5 xx

Lisa: Can't come round tonight. Have to work. Will is busy tonight. He told me not to call him. He must be studying. Maybe meet you next week. L. xxx

Day before murder.

Mum: Yes, of course Jenny can stay tomorrow night. I love having her here xx

Patrick: See you tomorrow

- What do you make of this? said Chris.
- Patrick! Patrick Blackburn!
- Did she know him?
- I didn't think so.
- It could be anyone named Patrick.
- I bet it's him.
- I'll make a note of the number and we can check.

Chris scrolled further down the texts. Nothing interesting. Into last week. Nothing. Previous week. Still nothing. Last month. Stop. Chris saw a name he recognised.

Will: Fuck you bitch. You're going to get what's coming to you.

- Another threat from that bastard, seethed Emma.
- He had threatened both Tina and Penny.
- And now they are both dead. He fits the profile. He knows about Jack the Ripper and his father is a surgeon. I think we should tell the police.
- I don't know, said Chris pensively, - Certainly, he's a misogynist but is he a computer hacker.
- He could be, he's intelligent enough.
- I'm just not sure. On the rare occasions I had the misfortune to be in his company he never showed any interest in computers. In fact, quite the opposite, he sees computer programmers as geeks to be ridiculed.
- What then? said Emma exasperated. – Are we going to do nothing until another mutilated body turns up?
- No, defended Chris a little offended. – Just let me do some research on him first.

- You have until tomorrow evening. Then we go to the police.
- Ok, conceded Chris getting up to leave.

Emma just sat there with her arms tightly crossed and an angry look on her face. Chris left silently and disappointed - no kiss tonight.

Chapter 11

Chris woke up to a text from Emma.

Emma: *Sorry I was angry with you last night. I didn't mean to be. This whole thing is just getting to me. See you this evening. I'll come to the flat. XXXX*

Four kisses noted Chris with a radiant smile. He switched on his computer, he had to find out about Will Dumas.

Emma was in Professor Bury's room with Jane, Will and Liam.

- How was the meeting with Patrick? Liam asked Emma.
- It was quite interesting.
- Did you get any closer to solving the mystery of who was Jack the Ripper?
- Not really, Patrick said the police knew but covered it up. But I don't know why they would do that.
- Possibly to avoid embarrassment and scandal at their own incompetence. Did he talk about Batty Street?
- Batty Street?
- It is widely believed that Jack the Ripper was a lodger in Batty Street. Patrick believes this.
- He never said. I'll ask him at the next meeting.

At the end of the tutorial Emma approached Professor Bury.

- Professor, do you have a mobile number for Patrick. I wanted to ask him about the meeting last night.

- I'm afraid I don't and unfortunately he is away today and will not be back until tomorrow.
- That's ok. Nothing important.

Emma picked up her bag and walked into the corridor.

- I have his number, said Jane pulling out her phone. – I'll send it to you.
- Thanks, replied Emma.

She checked her phone as the text came through from Jane with a mobile number. That was lucky Jane had Patrick's number she thought as she walked away.

Chris had assembled all the information he could on Will Dumas. The Dumas family lived in a townhouse in Chelsea. They were affluent, his father being a Harley Street surgeon specialising in heart surgery and his mother a mathematics teacher at a private school. The family were originally from Montreal, Canada. His grandparents on his father's side had moved to London in the 1950s. Will was a bright boy who showed an interest in his father's work and it was felt he would follow in his footsteps but instead chose to study psychology. On his Facebook page were pictures of him with various women. In fact, most of his Facebook "friends" were women. That did not surprise Chris.

School boy Will was a high achiever. He had been captain of the rugby team and achieved three A levels in Psychology, Biology and English. He had an offer to study at Jesus College, Oxford but chose UCL instead. He won a writing prize in his final year. The title of his essay: An Analysis of Jack the

Ripper. There was one more thing on his file. In his final year there was an allegation of sexual assault.

Chris had to admit there was a lot of circumstantial evidence surrounding Will Dumas. Maybe Emma was right and it was time to inform the police before there were any more killings.

****

Saucy J: Hi Valkyrie xx

Valkyrie: Hi xx

Saucy J: What are you up to?

Valkyrie: Nothing special.

Saucy J: Me neither. I wonder how we can alleviate our boredom xxx

Valkyrie: It's a problem isn't it? Xx

Saucy J: Would you like me to visit you and we can be bored together.

Valkyrie: That would be nice xx

Saucy J: I'll come this evening. Send me your address.

Jane texted her address and opened her draw pulling out black stockings and suspenders. She was just about to shower when the intercom buzzer sounded.

****

Emma had spent the rest of the day in the library researching the case of Jack the Ripper. There was a lot of information on the suspects, the victims and their histories. There were detailed accounts of the murders and the investigations. Emma compiled it all into a folder. She arrived at Chris's flat at 9.00pm with the folder under her arm. Chris opened the door. Emma entered smiling radiantly, she placed her hand tenderly on his arm and kissed him on the cheek.

- What's in the folder? asked Chris.
- Everything we will need.

Chris smiled recognising that these were the same words he had said to her last night when they went to Tina's flat.

- Where's Liam? she asked.
- He's been out most of the day.
- Where does he go? I know he was in the tutorial this morning. He was interested to know about Patrick's meeting.
- He said he was going to spend the evening in the library.
- I didn't see him, probably best he's out, we can work in private. What have you found out about Will?
- There is a lot of circumstantial evidence. He could have medical knowledge. I confirmed his father is a cardio surgeon. He has an A level at grade A in biology. I think it's highly likely he has dissected small animals, like frogs and rats.
- These skills could transfer to humans.
- He won a prize for and essay on Jack the Ripper.
- I remember he said he had an interest in the mystery before he came to university.
- There's something else, there was an alleged assault on a female pupil. The investigation seems to have been brushed under the carpet but I printed the report. Do you want to see it?

Chris gave Emma the printed page with the report. Emma read the title: Will Dumas - Allegation of sexual assault. She stopped and looked up. Then picked up her folder and quickly sifted through the pages.

- Here it is, she said triumphantly holding a sheet up. – It's only just struck me.
- What? said Chris expectantly.
- The name. Dumas. That was the surname of a prostitute that ripper suspect Francis Tumblety attempted an abortion on.

She moved her finger down the page and read:

- Francis Tumblety was arrested 23 September 1857 for attempting an abortion on a local prostitute named Philomena Dumas in Montreal.
- Montreal, I've got something on that, said Chris excitedly frantically searching his own papers. - The Dumas family moved from Montreal to London sometime in the 1950s.

They sat back to contemplate what they had. Certainly it was suggestive.

****

Jane had put on a silk red blouse leaving the top few buttons undone to give a tantalising glimpse of her cleavage. She had black stocking rolled up her shapely legs attached to a black suspender belt. A skimpy red thong and 6-inch stilettos completed the alluring ensemble. She had applied thick black mascara and even thicker scarlet lipstick to her full lips. She had lit two candles and placed them on either side of the bed. A bottle of red wine stood open on the bedside table. She had already had a couple of glasses and felt quite tipsy. The intercom rang.

- Come on up, she said pressing the door release.

She opened the flat door and left it ajar. Then she went into the bedroom and lay on the bed with a glass of wine in her hand and waited. She could hear footsteps approaching the front door. Then the door being pushed open followed by it firmly being closed. The anticipation heightened her excitement. She could hear the footsteps continuing down the hall getting nearer. Her door eased slowly open and a masked figure stood in the doorway.

****

- Even if Will Dumas is related to Philomena Dumas what does that prove? said Chris.
- That there is a link to Jack the Ripper.
- That's only true if Tumblety was Jack the Ripper.
- Patrick made a strong case for him. He had medical knowledge, he was a misogynist, he was known to be looking to buy uteri while in London in 1888 and after he fled to France on 24 November 1888 there were no more killings, the last one being Mary Kelly 9 November 1888.
- Ok. Even if Tumblety was Jack the Ripper. How does that connect to Will being the killer now?
- Revenge, ventured Emma
- For what? Jack the Ripper attempts an abortion on one of his ancestors and Will kills descendants of the victims of Jack the Ripper? It doesn't make sense.
- Ok, conceded Emma. – Maybe a bloodline directly from Jack the Ripper.

- How?
- Look it says it was an attempted abortion. Suppose the child born was Tumblety's.
- We are making a lot of assumptions here Emma, said Chris. - I just don't buy it.
- Have you got a better idea? challenged Emma.
- Let's put Will to one side for now. Did you get Patrick Blackburn's mobile number?

Emma reached into her pocket and produced her mobile phone

- Here it is, she said showing the display to Chris.

Chris picked up Tina's mobile and checked the numbers.

- It's the same. Did Professor Bury give you the number?
- No. Jane did.
- Jane? How did Jane have it.
- I don't know I suppose he must have given it to her.
- When? I thought she didn't know him.
- No. Well, only from a tutorial and the ripper meeting. She doesn't even like him.
- What's her surname?
- Ericsson, said Emma apprehensively.
- What information do you have on the next victim of Jack the Ripper?

Emma leafed through her folder again.

- Third victim, Elizabeth Stride. Born Elisabeth Gustafsdotter in a small village just north of Gothenburg, Sweden 27 November 1843. Moved to London some time in 1866. Married John Stride in 1869. He died in 1884 and she moved in with Michael

Kidney. She was killed 30 September 1888. Her body was discovered in Dutfield's Yard, just off Berner Street and Commercial Road, Whitechapel. Her throat was deeply gashed but no mutilation. It is believed the killer was disturbed by the arrival of a man driving a cart and pony entering the yard before he could remove any organs from the body.

- I was hoping that would be more helpful, said Chris disappointedly. – Let's look at the Ripper Club photo again.

They studied the photo. Four girls, two dead wearing clothing belonging to the victims of Jack the Ripper: Polly Nichols' bonnet and Annie Chapman's rings.

- We know the girl on the right is Tina and the girl centre left is Penny, summed up Chris
- Yes.
- Furthermore, the picture is titled the Ripper Club. I think it's not unreasonable to assume the other two girls are the next two victims.
- I think so too.
- But there were five victims in 1888. Where is the fifth girl?
- Perhaps there is no fifth girl, said Emma. – The last victim was Mary Kelly. She was young when she died and I cannot find any information of her having any children. But there's something else. The third and fourth victims, Elizabeth Stride and Catherine Eddowes, were killed on the same night.
- We need to identify the other two girls in the photo, said Chris urgently.

****

The masked figure moved towards Jane lying on her bed. He put his hand in his pocket and pulled out a length of rope. Jane looked at the rope.

- Mmmm I like role-play, she said seductively laying back on the bed.

The masked figure straddled her waist, gripped her wrists and pushed her arms roughly above her head.

- Not too rough, she said.

Her wrists were held together and she felt the rope being tied around them and pulled tight. She felt her arms being stretched back as the rope was attached to the headboard behind her. She was now totally powerless. He reached across to the bedside table and picked up her mobile phone and turned it off.

- That's better. Now we won't be disturbed, he said menacingly.

That voice, thought Jane, I know it.

- It's you!

She said no more as a cloth was shoved into her mouth.

****

Chris and Emma were studying the photo intensely. Four girls. They had identified Penny and Tina. Who were the other two? Lives depended on identifying them before it was too late.

- The girl centre right is impossible to identify with that shawl covering her whole head. I can't even see her hair, observed Emma. – It might not even be a girl.

- We should concentrate on the girl far left, replied Chris.

The girl on the left had a black fan in front of her face. She was wearing a short black jacket with a white blouse and a red skirt and black high heeled lace up boots. Around her neck was a red neckerchief.

- She could be anybody, observed Chris.

Emma stared at the girl. The more she looked the more she felt familiar. She looked somehow sluttier than the other girls. A red neckerchief?

- I've seen that red neckerchief before, she said suddenly.
- Where?
- In Bar Monte Carlo. Jane Ericson came in wearing it a few days ago.
- Ericsson, said Chris searching frantically through their research papers. – I've got it. Ericsson was the historic family name of Elizabeth Stride.

Emma hurriedly grabbed her phone and rang Jane's number. It went immediately to answer phone.

- She must have it turned off, said Emma.
- Do you know where she lives?
- Yes.

It was pitch black when they arrived at the modern block. Emma pressed the button for Jane's flat. No response. She pressed it again. No reply.

- She could be out, whispered Emma hopefully.
- Let's hope that's the reason, replied Chris.

He attached a device to the number panel at the front door. Emma watched and waited. She was getting used to Chris's devices now. The door opened and they went in.

- Best to use the stairs, advised Chris.

They made their way up the stairs to the third floor. Emma was aware of the quietness. The only sound was their own footsteps and her heart beating faster as they advanced. Maybe Jane was out. Maybe she was with Keith or another male friend. But why was her phone off? They arrived at the third floor. Emma could see Jane's door at the end of the passage. As she got closer time suddenly stood still. The door was ajar. She froze, unable to move, barely able to breathe. Chris turned and looked at her. Her face was white, her eyes fixed on the open door. Chris followed her gaze.

- Perhaps you should wait here, he said.
- No, she replied determinedly, - Like you said we are in too deep now to turn back.

She walked slowly past Chris towards the door steeling herself for whatever she might find inside. Chris followed as she approached the door at the end of the passage. She stopped outside the door and remained motionless. Chris stood behind her and waited. She could see the darkness through the crack between the door and the wall. She took a deep breath, stepped forward and pushed the door open. The light from the passageway partially illuminated the entrance hall. There was an open door far left from which was coming a flickering light.

- A candle, whispered Chris.

She moved steadily down the hall towards the flickering light. Her heart was accelerating faster with each step. She could hear her own breathing. She stopped again facing the bedroom door. This was it. No turning back. She gritted her teeth and with one sudden movement threw the door open. Immediately her hands covered her mouth to muffle her scream. Two candles almost burnt out, on either side of the bed lit up the body of a semi naked women. Her arms were pulled back and her wrists tied with rope to the headboard. The throat was cut and the face severely mutilated. Emma looked in horror at her blood-stained stockings. Her abdominal wall had been sliced down the middle and opened. Chris had found her phone and turned it on. He read the last texts.

- She was texting someone called Saucy J, he commented.
- It's a reference to a note Jack the Ripper sent to the police taunting them, she replied numbly, her eyes transfixed on the mutilated body. – He signed it Saucy Jacky,

She became aware of Chris opening drawers and rummaging through them.

- What are you doing?
- Looking for the red neckerchief?
- It's gone, isn't it? Just like the rings.
- I've found something else, he said suddenly and held up two wads of money. the bank notes held together by dark yellow bands.

Emma looked at the money.

- These are £50 notes. There must be a few thousand pounds here.

Emma was not listening. Something had drawn her attention to the body. She moved closer and picked up one of the candles. She leant over and held the candle close to the head to see better. The right side of the head was a bloody mess, but the candlelight allowed her to see. The right ear was missing. Just like Catherine Eddowes.

Chris and Emma went back to Emma's room in the halls of residence. She opened a bottle of wine and poured a large glass for herself and one for Chris. The room was small. A small single bed against the wall, a desk opposite with a wooden chair. The desk was covered in papers and books, a laptop and a small reading lamp. Chris sat at the chair and studied the papers. They were all about Jack the Ripper – victims, suspects, even a map of Whitechapel dated 1888. Emma was clearly as preoccupied with all this as he was. She walked towards him carrying two large glasses of wine and put one in his hand.

- God, what a night, she said sitting on the bed and taking a big gulp from the glass.
- Well, we know the third victim now, appraised Chris.
- There was something strange about that.
- What?
- The right ear had been sliced off.
- Why is that strange? he removes body parts.
- Yes, but Jack the Ripper removed the ear from Catherine Eddowes, the fourth victim, not the third, Elizabeth Stride.
- What does that mean? Has there been a killing we are unaware of?
- Catherine Eddowes and Elizabeth Stride were killed on the same night. It is believed that Jack the Ripper was

disturbed after killing Elizabeth Stride and did not have the time to mutilate the body so killed Catherine Eddowes and removed her ear which he later sent to the police.

- So what are you saying?
- Well, that Jack the Ripper failed to mutilate Elizabeth Stride in the way he intended so was forced to kill Catherine Eddowes. Suppose this killer is not only copying the ripper killings but eradicating the perceived mistakes.

Emma lifted the glass to her lips and drank the rest of the wine. Chris got up and picked up the bottle. He walked towards Emma and filled her glass and then his own. He sat down beside her. Even with everything that had happened tonight he was still enchanted by her.

- It would explain why there are only four girls in the Ripper Club photo, she said taking a sip from her glass.
- Maybe, replied Chris watching the glass touch her alluring lips. – We need to identify the last girl in the picture.

Emma noticed him looking at her. Chris looked quickly away and took a sip from his glass.

- Yes, but not tonight, said Emma sweetly.

Chris turned his head towards her. Their eyes met and held. Emma leant forward and kissed him gently on the lips. Perhaps it was the wine, perhaps the emotion of the evening. As they kissed the horrors seemed to melt away. Chris had dreamt of this moment. Emma's lips were as soft and sweet as he had imagined. Emma lay back on the bed.

- Stay with me tonight, she whispered.

Patrick sat in his college room with a large glass of bourbon. On the desk was a black metal box clamped and locked with a thick padlock. He looked pensively at the box. He lifted the glass and drank the bourbon in one huge gulp. Then he took the key from his pocket and inserted it into the padlock. He paused, moments like this were to be savoured. He turned the key slowly in the lock and gripped the lid firmly on both sides. It had all been worth it. He raised the lid and pushed it back on its hinges. Inside the box was a black bonnet, three bars rings and a red neckerchief.

Chapter 12

Chris sat in front of his computer. He was staring intensely at the Ripper Club photo. His mind kept wandering to the previous evening and Emma. It had been magical, perhaps the emotion of finding Jane dead had heightened everything and made it all much more intense. Chris had woken with Emma in his arms. Even asleep she was beautiful, breathing gently with her warm body against his. When she awoke she smiled sweetly and kissed him gently. She had to go to college but said she would come to his flat after that. Chris was counting down the minutes. He stared at the picture and with a great effort forced his mind to focus. Who was the fourth girl? The news of Jane's murder had been on the morning news, the police being informed by a neighbour who had discovered the door open. There was no mention of any other girls being killed. This was the first departure from the killings of Jack the Ripper who had killed two in the same night. Also, he had removed Jane's ear which in 1888 had happened to the fourth victim, Catherine Eddowes, not the third, Elizabeth Stride. However, Jane was connected to Elizabeth Stride through the name Ericsson. He looked at the picture. Four girls. Chris thought hard. If Elizabeth Stride and Catherine Eddowes are conjoined and attributed to Jane Ericsson that leaves the remaining girl in the picture, the one with the beige shawl over her head to be connected to the last victim in 1888. Chris opened the research folder Emma had compiled. He scanned down the name of the victims. Mary Kelly, the last victim of Jack the Ripper. He went to the notes on Mary Kelly and read.

Almost everything that is known about her came from Joseph Barnett, who she lived with prior to her death.

Born Mary Jane Kelly in 1863 in Limerick, Ireland but moved to Wales as a young child

Very attractive, 5ft7, blonde hair, blue eyes and a fair complexion

In 1879, at the age of 16, she married a collier named Davies. He was killed in an explosion two years later. There was a suggestion there might have been a child in this marriage.

She moved to London in 1884 where she worked as a high-class prostitute in the West End. During this time, she frequently rode in a carriage living the life of a lady and accompanied one gentleman to Paris. She did not speak much about her experiences in Paris but Barnett had the impression something had happened and she returned several months later.

She was a different person. She started drinking heavily and went from being a high-class escort in the West End to a cheap whore in the East End.

On Wednesday 7 November1888, two days before her murder, Mary was seen in Miller's Court, Whitechapel, by Thomas Bowyer, a pensioned soldier. She was talking to a well-dressed man. Bowyer noticed him because of his smart appearance. He had a long white collar which came down over the front of his long black coat and white cuffs protruding from the sleeves. The description closely resembled one given of a man seen with Elizabeth Stride just prior to her death.

On the night of the murder, Friday 9 November, George Hutchinson, resident in Whitechapel, was walking home down Commercial Street. As he passed Thrawl Street he was aware of a figure stood in the shadows. There was something unnerving about the motionless silhouette and Hutchison hurried by.

At the corner of Dean Street, he met Mary Kelly who asked him to lend her money but he had none to give her. She told him she must get money and walked towards Thrawl Street. Hutchinson watched her walking away. As she arrived at the corner of Thrawl Street the figure stepped out of the shadows and put his hand on Kelly's shoulder. Stood under the streetlamp Hutchison had a better view of him. He was wearing a black top hat, a long dark coat trimmed in astrakhan, a white collar with a black necktie. He wore dark spats over light button boots and had an expensive looking gold chain on his waist coat. On his hands he wore white kid gloves and was carrying a small package. The stranger and Kelly walked off together down Commercial Street and turned into Dorset Street. Worried for Kelly's safety Hutchinson followed them down Dorset Street. They stopped in Miller's Court. Hutchinson watched them talking then the stranger put his arm around Kelly and kissed her. They entered the building together. Hutchinson waited for a while in Millers Court. Everything was quiet and still. Not a sound could be heard. The light of a candle flicked in the window of Mary Kelly's room. Hutchinson felt a cold chill and pulled his coat tighter before heading out of Millers Court and going home. It was 3am.

The following afternoon police broke into Mary Kelly's room. Her clothes were neatly folded and placed on a chair with her boots in front of the fireplace. The walls around the bed were splattered with blood and in the middle of the blood-soaked sheets lay the naked body of Mary Kelly. Her face had been mutilated beyond recognition. The abdomen had been sliced open and removed and her breasts had been cut off.

Chris sat back in his chair unable to read any more. This was horrific. He was not unduly sensitive but he found reading about this killing distressing. He had to force himself to return to the text and began to write down the names and make notes. The last girl in the picture had to be identified.

George Hutchinson, who was probably the last person to see Mary Kelly alive.

Joseph Barnett, had lived with Mary Kelly just prior to her murder.

Davies, married Mary when she was 16.

Chris appraised the names: Barnett, Hutchinson, Davies. Liam Davies? Could he be linked to all this. There is no reason why the descendants could not be male, he thought. He looked at the photo again focusing on the figure under the shawl. The beige shawl covered the whole head and came down over the chest. Below the shawl the person was wearing a dark green ankle length dress from which protruded sturdy brown boots. The hands were not visible. He could be a male thought Chris. Liam was small and slight. Chris shook his head in disbelief, it was all too fantastic. He thought about the other girls in the photo: Jane Ericsson, Tina Stanley and Penny Holland. They all knew each other. It struck Chris as being highly probable the fourth person in the picture was also known to them.

Chris hacked into the university records. Davies, Liam.

He found his application form when he had applied to UCL.

Liam Tarquin Davies

Application to study Psychology

Qualifications: A levels: Computer Studies, Chemistry, Biology

Interests: Computer Programme design, online gaming

Work Experience: Mother is getting me work experience for the summer before starting university.

Not much help there thought Chris. He returned to the photo. There must be an object also. So far he had Polly Nichol's bonnet being worn by Penny Holland, Annie Chapman's three brass rings belonging to Tina Stanley, and Jane Ericsson with Elizabeth Stride's red neckerchief. Chris couldn't see anything on the fourth person. That bloody shawl is obscuring everything thought Chris frustrated. It must be something hidden out of view he concluded.

Bleep. A text message appeared on his mobile phone.

Emma: *Working at Bar tonight. Ripper meeting tomorrow at 6. I think you should come. XXX*

Emma was working in the bar that evening but finding it difficult to concentrate. She could not get the image of Jane's mutilated body covered in blood and the red stained walls out of her mind. The image of the sliced off ear was burnt into her memory. Then there was the missing red neckerchief. The killer must have it along with the other objects from the victims. Find the objects and you would find the killer, she decided. Then she thought about Chris and the night they had spent together. Maybe it was the emotion of everything but he was different to other boys she had known.

- Em!
- Em!

Emma suddenly became aware of someone calling her name.

- Em!

She looked up and saw Lisa standing by the cellar door struggling with empty crates.

- I've been calling you for ages, she said laughing. – You are miles away.
- Sorry, she said racing over and taking a crate off her.
- These need to go to outside.

They walked into the cellar and opened the back door. Outside was dark and cold. They put the crates down by the wall.

- What were you so deep in thought about? asked Lisa
- Oh, nothing, replied Emma who had no intention of telling her about Jane.
- It must be something, said Lisa pressing but laughing.

Emma decided she had to say something.

- Chis stayed at mine last night.
- Ooooo tell me all, said Lisa excitedly.
- It was nice.
- Are you going out together now?
- Maybe, I don't know, said Emma uncertainly.
- We can go out as a foursome. You know, with Will too.

We'll look forward to that, thought Emma dubiously.

- We'll see, she said diplomatically.

Suddenly her attention was drawn to something moving in the dark.

- There's someone there, she whispered.
- Where?
- There, she said pointing into the shadows.
- I can't see anyone.

Emma stepped closer. Nothing. She walked further forward, her heart starting to beat faster. She was certain she had seen a figure in the shadows. She kept moving slowly down the yard in the darkness. She stopped and listened. Silence. Her eyes scanned around. Nothing was moving. Suddenly she felt a hand on her shoulder and turned around in terror.

- Let's go back in. I'm getting cold.

She let out a huge sigh of relief looking into Lisa's face. They walked back to the building. At the door Emma glanced back into the yard, she was certain she had seen someone. She closed the door behind her. In the yard a figure emerged from the shadows.

Chapter 13

The following evening Chris was waiting for Emma in the Psychology department just before 6.00pm to go to the ripper meeting. He had not seen her since they spent the night together and was unsure of the situation between them. Was it a one off initiated by the trauma of finding Jane dead? Chris hoped not, that would make their relationship awkward. He was making himself paranoid. This was not like him. He was normally well balanced and clear thinking. Is this what love does to you? He heard footsteps and looked up to see Emma approaching. She seemed more beautiful than ever with a radiant smile. She gave him a hug then kissed him on the lips instantly dissolving all his doubts and fears. His calm and clarity returned to him as they walked towards Patrick's room

- Why did you want me to come to this meeting?
- I didn't. Patrick did.
- Patrick?

The door opened and Patrick stood before them. Chris observed him. He was in his usual black shirt, trousers and boots. Around his neck hung a silver chain with a strange star shaped pendent coming down below his chest. Chris and Emma entered the room and sat down. They were the only ones present.

- So, you're Chris Walker, said Patrick examining him intensely with his piercing eyes.
- Yes, replied Chris cautiously.
- I understand you're an expert in computing.

- I'm not sure you'd call me an expert, said Chris modestly unsure where this was leading.
- And a hacker

Chris remained silent. This was not a topic he wanted to discuss with a stranger.

- You don't need to be so defensive, continued Patrick. – You're just the person I've been looking for. No doubt Emma has informed you what I do.
- Research on Jack the Ripper, replied Chris.
- More than that. I'm seeking to solve the ultimate puzzle. I want to unmask Jack the Ripper.
- Why do you need me? asked Chris perplexed.
- Through my research I have discovered the existence of a report. This report was written in 1888 by Assistant Commissioner Sir Melville Macnaghten. In it lies conclusive proof of the identity of Jack the Ripper. He claims he destroyed all the ripper documents but if I'm right, and I believe I am, the report still exists and is on file at Scotland Yard. I want you to find this report.
- Even if I am a hacker, said Chris guardedly, - Hacking into Scotland Yard would be very difficult and dangerous.
- I'll pay you, said Patrick.

He stood up and walked to the filing cabinet, took a key from his pocket and opened the top drawer. Reaching inside he lifted out a brown paper package. He returned to the desk and put the contents on the desk. A wad of £50 bank notes tied with a dark yellow band.

Chris and Emma looked at the bundle of notes and the dark yellow band. Exactly the same as they had seen only hours before at Jane's flat. Emma was about to speak but Chris subtly shook his head and she stayed silent.

- I must go now, said Patrick. – Will you search for the report?
- I'll, need to think about it, replied Chris, his mind focused on the dark yellow band.

Emma remembered her conversation with Liam.

- What do you know about Batty Street? she asked
- In 1888 there was a lodger resident at 22 Batty Street. He disappeared after the five Whitechapel killings.
- Was he Jack the Ripper?
- I think he was, said Patrick decisively. – The house still exists.

They fell silent.

- I must go now, said Patrick. – We will meet again soon.

They returned to Chris's flat.

- What do you make of the bank notes tied with the dark yellow band in Patricks room? asked Emma.
- It was exactly the same as the ones we found in Jane's flat.
- Why would he kill them and leave money? It doesn't make sense.
- We know he knew Tina; he had sent her a text arranging to meet her on the day she was killed.

- He also knew Jane, she even had his telephone number, added Emma.

Chris had made his decision. He linked his code breaker to the computer. This was going to take a while. Scotland Yard would not be easy to hack into. There was also the danger that his hack would be traced.

****

Lisa was in the cellar at Bar Monte Carlo. The cellar was cold and dimmer than usual, the last remaining bulb had gone meaning the only light was provided by the door to the bar. She made her way carefully through the cellar carrying an empty crate and out into the yard. As she crossed the yard a figure watched her from the shadows. She put the crate against the wall and turned to walk back. Abruptly she stopped, she thought she could hear something. She peered carefully into the shadows. She hated being alone in the dark. What was that? She could hear it moving, getting closer. Suddenly, something leapt out from between the boxes.

- Oh, it's just you Suki, she said relieved.

She picked up the cat and went back inside.

****

It was past midnight and Chris was still trying to hack Scotland Yard.

- We still haven't identified the last girl in the photo either, said Emma looking at a print of the Ripper Club photo.
- If it is a girl, replied Chris.

- She's wearing a dress, said Emma pointing at the photo.
- Look closely. You can't see the face or head. It could be male.

Emma looked closely. Chris was right. There was nothing to prove definitively that it was female. Three dead girls and one person unidentified. Could be male or female. The beige shawl making identification impossible. She looked closely at the shawl inspecting it in minute detail. It hung down to the person's waist crumpled at the bottom. Then she noticed it was torn. A small strip had been ripped off it. She thought hard – a beige shawl with a strip torn off it.

- I've got it! shouted Emma suddenly, breaking the silence. – Catherine Eddowes shawl!

Chris was already searching for the information on Catherine Eddowes. He removed a page from the folder and read.

- Catherine Eddowes born 14 April 1842 in Graisley Green, Wolverhampton. Moved to Whitechapel in 1881 and resided at Cooney's Lodging House, 55 Flower and Dean Street. Her mutilated body was discovered in Mitre Square, Whitechapel 30 September 1888, the fourth victim of Jack the Ripper.
- Yes, and a fragment of the shawl was torn off by Jack the Ripper after her murder and found in Goulston Street, Whitechapel below the scrawled message on the wall "*the Jews are the men that will not be blamed for nothing*".
- Good work Emma. Now we know the artefact the killer is after.

- What about the people in her life? said Emma excitedly.
- She was also known as Kate Kelly. She met John Kelly, in 1881 when she moved to Whitechapel.
- And before that?
- She had three children in Wolverhampton with a retired soldier named Thomas Conway.
- Conway! That's it, she said hurriedly. – Lisa's surname is Conway.

She frantically picked up her phone and rang Lisa's number. The phone rang out again and again with no answer.

- On my God, there's no reply, said Emma wildly.
- Where is she tonight?
- She will be at the bar, replied Emma heading for the door.

Chris picked up the photo and his hacking device before following her.

****

The doors at Bar Monte Carlo were closed. The bar was empty except for Lisa, who was tidying up, Phil, the bar man, Keith and a girl in a mini skirt and crop top that he had been plying with drink all night. His hands were all over her and she seemed to be enjoying the attention.

- Keith, I need to go, said Phil
- That's fine, Phil, replied Keith undistracted from the scantily clad girl on his lap. – Lisa can lock up.

Phil left and Keith and the girl ambled across the bar. Lisa watched them disappear down the stairs into the cellar. She continued wiping down the tables then went to the front doors. As she locked the doors she looked through the glass. It was pitch black outside the only illumination being provided by the streetlamp opposite. She pressed the button beside her and the metal shutter rolled slowly down the outside of the doors. As they reached her eye line she saw a figure standing under the streetlamp opposite. The shutter came down and blocked her view. She lowered her head for another look. The figure was gone. The shutter reached the floor. Lisa went to the bar and sat on a stool. She hoped Keith would not be long. She did not like being alone in the bar. Everything was quiet. She could not hear anything from the cellar despite the door being open. Suddenly she heard footsteps on the pavement outside. The steps were moving towards the front door. They stopped. Lisa listened intensely. All was quiet. She looked around the deserted bar. Everything was still. Suddenly the shutters started to rattle. Lisa jumped off the stool in her fright covering her mouth to muffle her scream. The footsteps were moving away. Lisa was relieved to hear them getting fainter, now desperate to go home. She walked to the cellar door and stopped at the top of the stairs. Looking down into the cellar. all was dark and quiet.

- Keith! she called

No reply

- Keith! she shouted louder.

Still no reply.

She reached for the light switch and flicked it on. Nothing. She flicked it up and down again. Nothing.

- Keith! she shouted making her way tentatively down the stairs in the darkness.

Silence.

She reached the bottom.

- Keith! Are you there! I want to go home!

Nothing.

She moved carefully across the cellar passing the beer barrels and crates. It was so dark and cold. She turned a corner and could see the back door open. Suddenly, the cellar door to the bar closed behind her.

- Keith! she screamed hysterically wheeling around.

Footsteps were coming down the stairs.

- Keith!

As the footsteps got closer she could see the outline of a figure coming towards her. She was paralysed with fear, unable to move. The dim light caught the metal and she saw a glimpse of the blade in his hand.

- Please don't hurt me, she whimpered as tears began to roll down her cheeks.

The figure moved closer and closer. Suddenly she felt a hand grab her from behind and push her roughly aside. Lisa lay sprawled on the ground looking up at two silhouettes standing still facing each other. They both rushed forward, falling against the crates causing them to come crashing to the floor. Lisa screamed, got up and ran up the stairs. She closed the cellar door and locked it. In the bar the front door shutters were rattling ferociously.

- Lisa! Lisa!

She curled up into a ball sobbing uncontrollably.

- Lisa! Lisa!

That voice. She knew that voice. Emma. Behind her the cellar door handle was turning back and forth violently. She got up and raced to the front door. Still the cellar door handle was rattling. She pressed the button and the shutter began to rise slowly. Over her shoulder she could see the cellar door shaking and hear the furious bangs. The shutter came up. Through the glass she could see Emma. The doors opened and she rushed out sobbing into Emma's waiting arms. Chris ran past them into the bar towards the cellar door which was now silent. He opened the door. Removing a torch from his pocket he shone it down the stairs and made his way down. He shone it around the cellar. Empty crates and smashed bottles were scattered around the floor. Suddenly, he heard groaning. He moved slowly forward targeting the torch beam in the direction of the sound. There was a body on the floor. He approached and knelt down. He shone the torch into the face of the prostate figure.

- Patrick!

Chris moved the torch down his body and could see his hands on his stomach and blood-soaked shirt.

- We'll get help, said Chris. - Emma!
- You've got to stop him, said Patrick gripping Chris's arm.

- Who is he?
- I don't know his identity, but I can tell you about him.

Emma entered the cellar with Lisa following terrified.

- Patrick! she exclaimed seeing him on the floor.
- He saved me, wailed Lisa.
- Call for an ambulance, said Chris.

Emma took out her phone. Patrick continued.

- I knew he would attack her.
- She's the fourth girl, said Chris. – Descendent of Catherine Eddowes and possessor of her shawl.
- Yes, said Patrick a little surprised at how much Chris knew.
- He is killing them one by one by one for the possessions.
- No. You've got that wrong. He doesn't want the possessions. I have the possessions.

Chris was taken aback. He contemplated the situation. Patrick had the possessions. The money. Patrick had been in contact with Tina and Jane just before they were killed.

- You bought them.
- Yes. I'll tell you the whole story. When I was still in America I was contacted by someone in London doing research on Jack the Ripper. We emailed for a while and worked together on identifying the descendants of the victims of Jack the Ripper. He suggested I came to London and we continued working on the identifications here although we never met. Together we identified four but when we could not uncover the fifth he started to act erratically. He accused me of

withholding information and his emails became threatening. I stopped working with him.

- What name did he use in the emails? asked Chris
- JACK1888

Chris and Emma exchanged knowing looks. JACK1888.

- Why didn't you help the other girls? asked Chris.
- It wasn't until Jane was killed that I realised he was killing them. He was clearly waiting until I bought the possession. That was his signal to attack. So I didn't approach Lisa for the shawl but watched over her instead.
- You were the figure I saw in the yard last night, said Emma.
- Yes, I wanted to protect her from him. I knew he would get impatient and he did.
- Who is the fifth girl? asked Chris.
- I don't know, replied Patrick. – Neither does he but he will be trying to identify her. There's something else. He believes himself to be the descendant of Jack the Ripper. You have to get the secret report at Scotland Yard.
- Is he the direct descendent of Jack the Ripper?
- No. He is psychotically delusional and dangerously so.
- One more thing, have you ever seen this before?

Chris reached in his pocket and showed Patrick the picture.

- The Ripper Club? said Patrick. – No, I've never seen it before.
- I have, murmured Lisa. – I'm in it.
- I know, replied Chris. - What can you tell me about it?
- It was a fancy-dress party.

- Where? probed Chris.
- I can't remember, sobbed Lisa.
- Please try Lisa, begged Chris.
- I remember it was an old terraced house in Whitechapel.
- Batty Street? suggested Patrick.
- Yes, I remember now, Batty Street.

Chris looked at Patrick.

- It's got to be 22 Batty Street, said Patrick.

Chris stared at the picture then back at Lisa.

- Do you know who lives here? he asked her urgently.
- No.
- Who invited you?
- I received a card in the post. I was asked to wear the shawl.

This was all making sense to Chris. With Patrick's help someone had identified the descendants of the victims of Jack the Ripper, or at least four of them, and their belongings. He studied the picture once more. What was he not seeing? Then it struck him.

- Who took the photo?
- I didn't know the person, he was wearing a black cloak, a top hat and a mask.

Was this the serial killer they were searching for?

- I remember his name now, said Lisa.

All eyes were on her.

- Jack

Outside they could hear the sirens approaching. Patrick lunged forward and grabbed Chris's sleeve.

- You have to go to 22 Batty Street tonight, he implored.

Chris looked up at Emma.

- You stay here.

Emma threw her arms around him and embraced him tight.

- Please be careful, she pleaded as they parted

He handed the torch to Emma and went quickly out through the back door.

It was pitch black when Chris arrived in Batty Street, a derelict place with hardly any lighting. He stood in the deserted street surrounded on both sides by the shabby, antiquated terraced houses, remnants of another time. In the dark he struggled to see the numbers, he would have to use his phone for illumination. He felt the cold winter air cutting through his clothes as he walked, carefully examining each house. Then there it was, two rusted metal numbers nailed to the door, 22. 22 Batty Street. The window beside the front door was boarded up. He had to get inside. The boards seemed to have been up for some time, they looked worn by the rain and wind and broken at the bottom right corner. Chris grabbed the edge and tugged it hard. A piece came away in his hand. The wood was damp. He pulled another piece away then another until there was a hole large enough for him to squeeze through. He put his head through the gap and crawled inside.

The dank smell hit him immediately. He shone his phone around the barren room and the dust covered bare floorboards. Surely, no-one lived here, he thought. He moved carefully towards the stairs. The bannister was broken and the steps creaked as he ascended. On the landing were two opposing closed doors. He opened the first and was greeted with the same stench of dry-rot and dust he had experienced downstairs, quickly closing the door and moving to the other. He turned the handle. Locked. He turned to the side and put his shoulder against the door and pushed. Nothing. He slammed hard against the door. There was a slight movement. He kept doing it until he heard the crack of the lock breaking. Pushing the door open he looked into the darkness. He shone his phone around the room. No dust and no smell. There was a small bed on the right strewn with papers and photos. Against the back wall was a desk and chair both similarly covered in papers and photos and a laptop still switched on. Someone had been here and recently. Chris moved forward and examined the photos. There were old black and white photos of women that by now he was familiar with. He picked one up, it was the mutilated body of Mary Kelly. Looking down he recognised other photos – Polly Nichols, Annie Chapman. There were also more recent colour photos. Chris sifted through them. He picked up a photo that made his blood freeze. It was a picture illuminated by candlelight of Jane Ericsson's bloody corpse tied to the bed exactly the same as he had found her that night in her flat. There were other recent pictures. He found one of Penny Holland lying dead in Regent's Park and another of Tina Stanley's bloody corpse on the hall floor where she was killed. They were all here, macabre souvenirs for their killer. . He went quickly to the desk, knocked the papers off the chair and sat down. The screen was displaying Scotland Yard and a list of files marked Top Secret. Chris recognised a hack when he saw one. The hack had already got quite far. He went to the search history, what was he looking for? There it was, Ripper Murders, Case Closed, 20 December 1888. He found the file and clicked it. A password box appeared on the screen. Chris quickly attached his hacking device. Whoever it was had clearly been unable to break the code. Turning around Chris became aware of a shelf on the wall behind. He stood up and moved towards it. There were jars lined up along it. As he approached them he flinched in horror. They were human body parts, internal organs. Chris scanned his eyes along the shelf going from jar to jar. He stopped and stared into the last one and was immediately filled with anger and revulsion as he looked at the severed ear inside. The killer was operating out of this room. He sat on the bed and sifted through the scattered papers. One drew his attention. He picked it up.

Polly Nichols	*Penny Holland*	*Bonnet*
Annie Chapman	*Tina Stanley*	*3 Brass Rings*
Elizabeth Stride	*Jane Ericsson*	*Red Neckerchief*
Catherine Eddowes	*Lisa Conway*	*Beige Shawl*
Mary Kelly	*?*	*?*

Mary Kelly, also known as Marie Jeanette Kelly, Ginger, Fair Emma.

No. It couldn't be. Emma. Suddenly, he heard a buzzing from the computer and returned speedily to the screen, ACCESS GRANTED. Chris opened the file and read.

Letter from Detective Inspector Abberline to Assistant Commissioner Sir Melville Macnaghten

There will be no more murders in Whitechapel, the matter is at an end. It was found at 22 Batty Street as expected. The last one was indeed a tragedy, to kill the mother of your child. The child has been put into care. I might be sentimental, but I left the locket with the child. In years to come it will not be important. I doubt the photos will even be recognised.

Chris rapidly sifted through the photos. He recognised them as the victims of Jack the Ripper. He was looking for Mary Kelly. He found her. A photo taken before her death. She had been a beautiful young woman dressed in white full-length dress tied with a belt. Around her neck hung the locket, a locket Chris had seen many times before. He was transfixed, not hearing the footsteps behind him and the sudden blow to the head. He slumped to the ground unconscious. His assailant read the letter on the screen and looked at the photo. He removed Chris's phone and texted.

Chris: *Where are you now?*

Emma: *Back in my room*

Chris: *I'm on my way.*

Emma: *OK. I'll leave the door open for you xx*

He put a small black leather bag on the table. He opened it and put the phone inside next to a long thin bladed knife.

****

When Chris came around he was lying in the dark. He clambered into the chair holding his head. Reaching into his pocket and discovered his phone gone. He had to focus, quickly turning to the computer and hacking his mobile phone. He read the texts with horror, he had to get to Emma before it was too late.

It had been a long exhausting evening. Emma lay on the bed. She felt totally drained with the emotion of the night. Lisa had been attacked, Patrick had been stabbed but would live and Chris was on the killer's trail. She was so tired she could barely keep her eyes open. She switched off the light and closed her eyes. Everything was quiet and still.

****

She had no idea how long she had been asleep when she was awoken by the door closing. She heard the footsteps coming towards her.

- Chris?

No reply.

The figure came closer. Suddenly she felt unnerved. She reached over and turned on the bedside lamp. She looked in terror at the masked figure and saw the blade above his head. As the blade came down she rolled to the side. The blade cut through the sheet and ripped into the mattress. Emma jumped up and ran to the door. Locked. She fumbled frantically with the locks, pulling the bolt back, undoing the chain and turning the handle. Suddenly a hand grabbed her hair from behind and dragged her to the floor. She reached around and tried to free herself but he as too strong. She was flipped onto her back struggling desperately against her unknown assailant. He straddled her stomach pinning her down. She lashed out and ripped the mask from his face. For an instant time stood still as she looked up in stunned disbelief into the face of a killer.

- Liam?
- You're the last one fair Emma, he said menacingly. – I'm going to cut you up just like Mary Kelly.

She tried to wriggle free but he was too powerful. He gripped her wrists in both hands and pinned them down behind her head. She was totally helpless. He crossed her wrists and held them with his left hand. With his right hand he picked up the knife and lifted it high in the air. Emma could see the long thin blade glistening. Suddenly, the door burst open. Chris rushed in and grabbed Liam's arm causing the knife to fly across the floor. Chris pushed him off Emma falling on top of him. Emma wriggled free as Chris and Liam grappled against each other. Liam over-powered Chris getting on top of him, putting his hands around his throat and pressing hard. Chris fought to get free but in vain. The colour was draining from his face as his last breath was being squeezed out of his body. Suddenly the squeezing stopped, Chris could see the agonised look in Liam's eyes. Liam staggered to his feet and turned towards Emma. Her hand was clenched tight around the knife, along its thin blade was a line of bright red blood. The blood stain was spreading across Liam's back. He fell to the floor. His body shuddered as the blood formed a pool below him then was still.

Chris looked at Liam's lifeless body and thought about what he knew about him. His mother had got him a summer job prior to starting university and she was a nurse at the local hospital. That is when he must have learned about anatomy and dissection. All that time Liam was supposedly working on a computer game in the library he was really at 22 Batty Street identifying the ripper descendants to carry out his warped plan of mirroring the killings. That's why Emma had not seen him in the library. He looked at Emma.

- Why me? she asked trembling.
- You're the fifth girl, replied Chris. - It's the locket.

Emma glanced down at the locket hanging around her neck. Chris approached her, reaching around her neck, unclipping the chain and removing the locket.

- Have you ever opened it? he asked.
- No. It doesn't open.

Chris gripped the locket and banged the clasp against the table until it broke.

- This is it.
- I don't understand, sad Emma perplexed.
- Emma, you're the descendent of Mary Kelly.

Emma was shocked, she slumped to the floor. Chris sat beside her and put the locket in her hand. She moved her fingers to open it when Chris put his hand over hers and stopped her.

- There's something more you need to know before you decide to open it, he said calmly and quietly. – There are two pictures in the locket. Mary Kelly accompanied an unknown man to Paris. The reason she was a changed person when she returned was because she gave birth to a child which she was forced to give up. It's from this child that you are descended. It's the reason she was killed all those years ago.

- What are you saying? said Emma trembling with the horrific realisation.
- The photos in the locket are Mary Kelly and the unknown man, the father of the child and her killer.

Chris removed his hand from Emma's. With trembling hands Emma put her fingertips on the broken clasp and slowly opened the locket. On the left was a beautiful young woman, Mary Kelly. Emma looked at the photo on the right. It was the photo of a man that she recognised.

- Jack the Ripper.

THE END

STRANGER IN THE NIGHT

Ross Conrad had dreamed of being a policeman ever since he could remember. As a child he loved playing cops and robbers, he was of course, always the cop. He had a plastic dome police helmet which was never off his head, a plastic truncheon and toy hand cuffs. The other children used to call him Bobby Conrad. He loved the police shows on television from The Bill to CSI. He had no time for the amateur detectives of fiction such as Sherlock Holmes or Miss Marple, these were fantasy creations who did not exist in real life and frequently painted the real police as fools instead of the highly skilled professionals that Ross knew them to be.

Ross grew up to be tall and slim with light brown hair that he always kept short and tidy. He was keen to leave school as soon as he could and join the police, but his parents insisted he went to university first, so he did. He did not overly care for being a student, but he did meet Becky. Becky was quite reserved when he had met her in first year. She was small and slim and Ross had been drawn immediately to her long flowing chestnut hair and coy smile. He was not very confident with girls but had plucked up the courage to ask her for a coffee. They talked easily on their date as though they had known each other for years and became an item on the campus. Ross loved Becky and Becky loved Ross in a way that only young 19-year olds can. They married a month after his graduation. It was a double celebration because Ross was accepted as a police cadet the same day as the wedding. They moved into a little semi-detached house together on a modern housing estate and Ross's life was going to plan. He shone at police cadet training school and was assigned to a station and partner. His partner and mentor was PC David McAdam, a highly experienced officer in his forties. McAdam lived with his wife Angela in a neighbouring street to Ross in a similar type of house. Angela was McAdam's second wife, small and slim and had long flowing hair like Becky. She was considerably younger than him, in fact about the same age as Ross himself. Living so close was quite advantageous as McAdam could pick up and drop off Ross in the patrol car.

On a cold dark winter's night as they were on patrol they came across a car seemingly abandoned in a deserted country lane on the outskirts of the city. The lane was narrow and surrounded by trees and bushes. There were no streetlamps with the only illumination being provided by the full moon above. McAdam slowed down as they passed and looking across could just about make out the silhouette of a figure in the driving seat. He pulled in just ahead of the lone car and turned the engine off. It was so quiet, eerily quiet, no sound from anywhere. No wind in the trees, no small animals moving in the bushes, nothing, just silence. He glanced in the rear-view mirror. The figure was motionless. Both officers got out of the patrol car to investigate. The night was so quiet and still they could hear each footstep as they walked and see the breath in front of their faces. As they approached the car Ross was struck by its strange shape. It was very low like a sports car but pointed at the front and raised at the rear. Ross was a car enthusiast and knew all the top sports makes but this was something different to anything he had seen before, reminiscent of an old Triumph TR7 but more pointed at the front. As they neared Ross could see that the car had no lights or registration plate. What kind of strange car was this? They reached the car and bent to look in the driver's window. Inside was a tall, scrawny man dressed in a long black robe with fine long white hair down to his waist. He remained still just facing forward. McAdam knocked on the window with his knuckles breaking the deathly silence.

The stranger moved his head slowly and looked at the officers. Ross observed his thin bony face and sharp pointed nose. There was something unusual about it, almost unnerving. He was struck by his pale and gaunt skin and his sunken lifeless eyes. It reminded him of a dead body he had once seen and sent a chill down his spine. The window began to wind down.

- Good evening sir. Can I ask what you are doing out here alone at this time of night? enquired McAdam in his usual authoritarian manner.
- Is it against your laws to be out alone at night? replied the stranger
- Is this your car sir?
- I've never understood this strange concept of ownership that you have.
- Can I see your licence please sir? said McAdam getting increasingly annoyed with the stranger's obtuse responses.

The stranger looked at Ross. Ross could feel his deathly eyes burning into his own.

- So, you're Ross Conrad

Ross was surprised to hear the stranger speak his name.

- Or do you prefer Bobby Conrad?

Ross had not heard this name since he was a young child

- Living out your dream of being a policeman and married to the lovely Becky.

Ross was unnerved that the stranger knew so much about him.

- Who are you? he blurted out in desperation.
- The question is not who I am, but what I am.

McAdam could see the increasing tension in the young officer's face.

- Name! he barked through clenched teeth.
- You would not understand my name

- Address!
- I am from no place known to you
- I've had enough. Show me your licence right now or you are going to spend the night in the cells.
- I have no need of a licence, laughed the stranger derisively throwing his head back.
- I'll play along, said McAdam switching his manner to patronise the stranger. - Where are you from?
- I am not of this world
- So, you're an alien?
- Something more than that
- A superhero? Do you have superpowers? asked McAdam mockingly.
- Perhaps you could call them powers.
- Give us a demonstration of your powers.
- You won't like it if I do
- I'll risk it, smirked McAdam

The stranger closed his eyes, a look of concentration on his face. He was still and solid, like rock, as though transfixed. McAdam laughed and looked at him incredulously. He glanced at Ross. Ross was not laughing. He looked worried. This weirdo had really got to him, thought McAdam, time to put a stop to this charade. Just as McAdam went to speak the stranger suddenly opened his eyes.

- It's done

He looked at the officers with his eyes seemingly more dead than before.

- Your wife is dead
- Becky! Ross cried out
- Out of the car right now, commanded McAdam angrily.

The stranger remained still. Ross was paralysed with desperation. McAdam had to snap Ross out of his state.

- PC Conrad get him out of the car right now, he ordered.

Ross's eyes were wild and panicked.

- PC Conrad get him out of the car. NOW!

Ross moved forward frantically grabbing the door handle and yanking it open. The stranger just sat there with an unnatural calmness. Ross reached in and grabbed him by the arm. As his fingers closed around the stranger's bony arm his mind went into a racing whirl. He felt as though he was racing across the land with the surroundings rushing past him in a blur. As everything stopped spinning and came into focus he found himself outside the house. In the street outside he saw a parked ambulance with its blue lights flashing. The house was in total darkness. His body seemed to elevate and glide through the front door into an eerily quiet hall. At the end of the hall he saw the kitchen door. He floated towards the end of the passage. The door opened and despite the darkness he could make out the figure of the body laying still on the floor with the long flowing hair covering the face.

- Becky! he wailed.

His vision blurred and his mind was spinning again. He was conscious of being back in the lane with McAdam pulling him back.

- It's Becky. I've got to get to Becky, he said trembling and attempting to break free from McAdam's grip.
- Go and sit the patrol car, said McAdam trying to maintain control of the situation.

Ross felt the grip release and ran to the squad car, stumbling as he did so.

- You, hissed McAdam at the stranger. - You just stay here. I'll be back.

He reached in and took the car keys out of the ignition. The stranger remained just as silent and still as always.

McAdam slammed the door shut and strode briskly back to the patrol car, opened the door and got in. Ross had his mobile phone clenched to his ear, a look of increasing terror on his face as the phone kept ringing out again and again. McAdam kept his attention on the car behind as he spoke.

- What the hell is wrong with you? You need to pull yourself together boy.
- I saw her. She's dead.
- No-one is dead.
- I saw her. There's no answer from her phone. I need to get home.
- No! Enough! shouted McAdam. - I'll tell you exactly what we are going to do. We are going to take that nutter to the station and he can spend the night in the cells.

He reached across and shook Ross roughly by the shoulders.

- Repeat it back to me. We are going to take him back to the station.
- We are going to take him back to the station, mumbled Ross.

They got out and walked back to the car. McAdam unclipped his handcuffs ready. He took a firm grip of the car door and opened it.

- You're going to……

He stopped speaking abruptly. The car was empty.

- Let's go, said Ross, panic taking over again.
- No. He must have got out.
- You were looking at the car the whole time, said Ross in desperation.
- He must have got out, repeated McAdam with less certainty.
- You know he never got out. But he's gone. Becky. I need to get home.

McAdam said nothing. He turned and walked hastily to the patrol car. They sped back to the city in silence save for the constant ringing out of Ross's mobile. Over and over again, a haunting ringing in the darkness with no-one to answer. Arriving outside the house Ross raced out even before the car had fully stopped leaving McAdam alone and silent.

The house was in darkness, not a single light to be seen. Ross ran to the front door. He yanked the keys out of his pocket and searched frantically for the right one, the keys spinning in his hand. Where was the front door key? The keys fell to the floor. He got on his knees and groped for them in the darkness. Where have they gone? He swept the ground with his hands. I have them. He bolted up and put the key in the lock throwing the door open.

- Becky!

Nothing.

- Becky!

He ran down the hall in darkness, not even stopping to turn on the light, he had to get to the end of the passage. At the door he put his hand on the handle, turned it and then stopped motionless. For the first time since he had met the stranger he stopped to think. He knew what he was going to find when he opened the door, he had already seen it. A life so idyllic was going to be shattered in seconds. His whole future lain to waste. He released the handle and took a step back. Ross did not want to see behind the door, he desired to turn and run. Yet he could not. He stood paralysed with fear and dread, not wanting to move forward, unable to move back. A force within him, outside of his will, moved his hand back onto the door handle. It compelled him to turn it. The door began to open. Gradually it opened, inch by inch. The inside was pitch black. He could not see, he did not want to see. His eyes scanned the floor. The invisible force within him moved his trembling hand slowly up towards the light switch. His finger paused over the it.

Click.

Nothing. The kitchen was empty. Suddenly he felt a hand on his shoulder. He spun round. He let out a wail and flung his arms around her.

- Becky! My Becky.

She held him tight as tears rolled down his cheeks.

- I thought I'd lost you forever.
- What's the matter? she asked tenderly caressing his hair. - Why is David McAdam sitting in the car outside?
- David! I forgot about David. Come with me, he said taking her by the hand and walking quickly to the front door.

He waved to McAdam from the front door with his arm around Becky, holding her tight. He had never known such intense emotion. McAdam drove away and they closed the door.

McAdam was pensive and unsettled as he drove the short distance home. He had been watching the deserted car the entire time. How did the stranger get out? He had just disappeared. Who was he? As he turned the corner into his street outside his house he saw the parked ambulance with its blue lights flashing.

Other Books

JACKPOT MILLIONAIRE

A J Boothman

Danny Taylor is a middle-aged, working-class bloke who dreams of a better life away from the drudgery of work and his mundane, repetitive existence. He fantasises about being rich and having fast cars and even faster women. All this could become a reality if only he could win the lottery. Would this really lead to the fantastic life he imagines?

Jackpot Millionaire is a fast-paced comedy.

Other Books

SHEER HATE

A J BOOTHMAN

The Vigil is a vicious online newspaper that revels in muckraking and delights in ruining lives, leaving a trail of victims in its wake with deadly consequences. Seductive reporter, Silky Stevens, and sleazy photographer, Frank Ebdon, will do anything to get a front-page story. Journalist, Nick Rose, struggles with his past, but is forced to use all his investigative skills to unmask a killer driven by sheer hate.

Includes the short suspense story “A Dark Winter’s Tale”.

Out Soon

THE RAVEN'S VENGEANCE

A J BOOTHMAN

Events from the past spawn great vengeance in the sleepy Irish village of Rathkilleen. To catch a killer Detective Teagan O'Riordan will have to discover the secret of the Raven.

"I WILL EXECUTE GREAT VENGEANCE ON THEM WITH WRATHFUL REBUKES; AND THEY WILL KNOW THAT I AM THE LORD WHEN I LAY MY VENGEANCE ON THEM."

EZEKIEL 15:17

Printed in Great Britain
by Amazon

42128217R00095